A REVELAT

James Graham caught
after she had gotten into bed.

"What are you doing in here?" Anna Lee hissed at him. "Get out of my bedroom."

"Why should it bother you?" he said bitterly. "I haven't noticed that you've been so particular lately."

"What are you talking about?" Anna Lee demanded.

"I followed you this afternoon."

"Why, you little sneak . . ."

"I think it's disgusting," he said. "How could you do such a thing? With a *half-breed*! You let him put his filthy, greasy, disgusting hands on you!"

"Stop it, James!"

"I won't," he said, his eyes glittering with hatred. "Don't you even know or care about your family? Even if you don't care about yourself, you should have some consideration for Mama and me!"

Overcome with anger, Anna Lee's words tumbled out before she had time to think. "Don't you know who *you* are?" she screamed. "Why, everybody knows that you—"

As she caught herself and stopped in mid-sentence, a deadly quiet enveloped the room.

"They know *what*?" James demanded. "What is it that everybody knows about me?"

The tears were welling up in Anna Lee's eyes. "Please . . ." she said. "Please don't—"

And James Graham turned and stalked out of the room without saying another word . . .

The Making of America Series

THE WILDERNESS SEEKERS
THE MOUNTAIN BREED
THE CONESTOGA PEOPLE
THE FORTY-NINERS
HEARTS DIVIDED
THE BUILDERS
THE LAND RUSHERS
THE WILD AND THE WAYWARD
THE TEXANS
THE ALASKANS
THE GOLDEN STATERS
THE RIVER PEOPLE
THE LANDGRABBERS
THE RANCHERS
THE HOMESTEADERS
THE FRONTIER HEALERS
THE BUFFALO PEOPLE
THE BORDER BREED
THE FAR ISLANDERS
THE BOOMERS
THE WILDCATTERS
THE GUNFIGHTERS
THE CAJUNS
THE DONNER PEOPLE
THE CREOLES
THE NIGHTRIDERS
THE SOONERS
THE EXPRESS RIDERS
THE VIGILANTES
THE SOLDIERS OF FORTUNE
THE WRANGLERS
THE BAJA PEOPLE
THE YUKON BREED
THE SMUGGLERS
THE VOYAGEURS
THE BARBARY COASTERS
THE WHALERS
THE CANADIANS

THE CANADIANS

Lee Davis Willoughby

A James A. Bryans Book from Dell/Emerald

Published by
Dell Publishing Co., Inc.
1 Dag Hammarskjold Plaza
New York, New York, 10027

ISBN: 0-440-00978-2

Printed in the United States of America

First printing—May 1983

1

SPRING came in its season to the Red River Settlement in that year of 1855: a Canadian spring, fresh and new and turbulent. Snowdrops brightened the sodden drabness of the muck and compost underfoot, green shoots came out of the ground and made their seasonal appearance on the end of shrub and tree branches. Their hue was as new as the new northwestern season: the tenderest, most delicate of greens.

The rest was turbulence and chaos. Roadways were awash with mud. Streams were swollen. Rough wooden bridges had given way. Rushing water had strained them beyond their limits; fallen limbs and rotted tree trunks carried by the current had battered them until they splintered. And the timbers from the ruined bridges had themselves become part of the destructive flotsam that was carried on downstream to wreak further destruction, flooding fields and taking down more bridges.

* * *

No one in the small cabin behind the backwoods general store knew for sure whether they were cut off completely from the rest of the world. Not the five-year-old girl with blue eyes, who had been told to leave the room, but who had crept back and now hung in the doorway, watching. Not the old woman with the one good eye and the strong, gnarled hands, who bustled back and forth between the bed and the kettle of hot water as it came to a boil on the black, cast iron stove.

And not the pregnant woman who lay on the bed, gripping the slats on either side as the pains started to come closer and closer together, refusing to cry out so she would not scare the little one, looking out at the hard rain that lashed its fury against the room's one small glass window.

Whether they were cut off or not, it hardly mattered at this point. They were on their own, whatever happened, and there would be no sending out for help if anything were to go wrong. It was thirty miles to the nearest town, and there was no chance of even a casual passerby dropping in at the store on a night like this. Whatever needed to be done, they would do it alone.

The wind knew the cabin with the familiarity of old enmity. The man who had built the cabin had chinked its walls and crannies with all the shrewdness that a man can bring to the wilderness, but the wind was shrewder by far, and it still found places to blow in, to send icy drafts scurrying across the floor and make the fire dance sudden crazy steps in the fireplace. The little girl had put more kindling on tonight, and the old woman had dragged extra logs in, to make sure that it was warm enough for the woman.

The midwife had been out with the woman for a week, waiting for the baby to have it's time. She had promised she would come, and one day the woman had driven into Kildonan to pick her up, while she still could.

She could still drive a wagon then, and the bridges had all still been standing; but the creek had been dangerously high, and she knew that for that reason and others, it would be unwise to wait any longer.

"I know that it's time," the woman had said, and the old woman had accepted that.

The old woman's name was Duoma. She was a *métis*, as they called themselves, or a *bois-brulé*, the people whose skin was the color of burnt wood. A half-breed, half Indian and half French-Canadian. She understood a great deal about feelings and hunches and instincts. And she knew that this woman, Anglo though she was, had been right about feelings before.

The woman's name was Charlotte Graham, and she ran the store near Lake Winnipeg, in that area of the North American continent which lay to the west of the borders of Lower Canada, and was known only as the Northwest. The Northwest had one populated area, the group of small communities and farms known as the Red River settlement, and Charlotte Graham's store was on the very outskirts of that settlement.

She lived there alone with her daughter, Anna Lee. The two of them had been alone since the death of Charlotte's husband nine months before.

Charlotte kept the store going by herself, as she had even before: her husband had been a fur trapper. Her business came from trappers, and from travelers and hunters and the occasional prospector. For the hunters and trappers there were bullets and steel traps; for the prospectors, pans and picks. For the travelers, there was beer and ale and whiskey, a warm fire and a pot of stew—buffalo, bear, caribou or whatever small game Charlotte had been able to bring down with the .30-.30 rifle she kept on the wall behind the counter.

For all, there were snowshoes, leggings and boots, chests of tea and coffee, boxes of tobacco, raisins, rice, loaf sugar. There were robes and blankets, moccasins and buckskin jackets embroidered with beadwork and dyed porcupine quills. And pemmican, made of strips of dried buffalo meat and hardened fat, the staple trail provision of the Northwest.

It was a meager living, but it was the life she had chosen for herself, and she did not complain.

She clenched her teeth, and gripped the sides of the bed again.

Douma stood over her, rocking back and forth with her shoulders.

"More pain?" she asked.

Charlotte nodded her head slightly, unwilling to risk the moan that might have escaped her lips if she had opened her mouth to talk.

Douma took in the information, and measured it in her head back against the time of the last contraction. She did not tell time in minutes, against some internal clock, and she knew just what each interval she counted meant. She placed her hand on Charlotte's stomach, first up high, then down low.

"Gonna be come soon. Ver' soon now. Mebbe dis be it," she said. "You feel better go ahead an' scream, go ahead an' cry."

Charlotte shook her head. The contraction passed, and she let out her breath in a harsh sigh.

She opened her eyes that had been shut to a squint, and saw Anna Lee standing in the doorway.

"I told you to scat," she said. "Now do as I say. Scat!"

Anna Lee disappeared from sight. Douma shook her head, but said nothing. A couple of minutes later, the child was back in the doorway. And Charlotte was going into another contraction.

"You doan wanna cry," Douma said. There was no rising inflection to her voice, but Charlotte understood it as a question, and nodded agreement.

"You tak dis, den," Douma said.

She reached into the worn leather pouch at her waist, and pulled out a leaden bullet. There were tooth marks on it already; it had seen service in the cause of Douma's midwifery before. She held it up to Charlotte's face, and Charlotte took it between her teeth.

Anna Lee took a couple of steps over the doorsill, further into the room, closer to the bed.

"Now get up," Douma said.

Charlotte rose up to her knees and, leaning forward, gripped the crossbeam of the bedpost. Douma would deliver the baby using a technique she had adapted from the method she had always used, the old Cree method of midwifery, practiced for hundreds of years in the buffalo-skin tipis of the prairie.

There, two wooden stakes were driven into the ground, the dirt floor of the tipi, and a third lashed between them. Handholds were whittled into the crossbar for the woman to clutch, while she dug her feet into the mat of moss on which she knelt.

For Charlotte, in 1853 and in a fur trader's cabin, the method was brought up to date. A straw-filled mattress had replaced the moss, but Douma had still notched the handholds into the crossbar of the frame, and Charlotte slipped her hands into them.

"Now push," Douma said.

Veins stood out on Charlotte's temples, sinews on her neck. Anna Lee, advancing yet another couple of steps closer, clenched her little fists in sympathetic support for her mother's effort.

Anna Lee stood openmouthed in wonder. Charlotte's jaws were still clenched rigidly, and her teeth were sunk into Douma's bullet.

For ten, fifteen, then twenty minutes she went on like that. Douma pressed Charlotte's stomach and sides with the palm of her hand, then with the heel. She muttered to herself in the Cree Indian tongue, and hummed an odd, soothing, singsong melody that sounded as old as the wind which still whistled and moaned all around them, and kept the fire in its flickering dance.

Charlotte kept straining. And when her muscles would weaken from the effort, Douma would let her relax for a few seconds only; then she would wipe the sweat from her forehead, and, rocking in uncanny rhythm with the new life struggling inside Charlotte, would tell her again, in her low, singsong voice:

"Is coming now. Push again."

Anna Lee was nearly up to the bedside now. She looked with great interest at her mother's face, contorted but silent, biting down on the bullet. Charlotte was completely unaware of her daughter's presence, even though Anna Lee was so near to her. Charlotte's eyes were open but filmed over, seeing only inward, as she brought all her concentration to bear on the effort to give birth to the new life within her.

Anna Lee moved down, closer to where Douma was standing. The midwife knew that she was there, but did not tell her to leave.

Anna Lee wanted to see it all. To see the baby being born, coming from out of that secret place between her mother's legs—that mystery place from which, as she vaguely understood, she must have come once upon a time, when she was as tiny as a newborn babe. That secret place that would be the same in her someday, if she were to grow up to be a mother, too.

It was clean and shiny and white, not dark as Anna Lee had somehow expected (she had no way of knowing that the midwife had shaved Charlotte befor her labor began, another trick that Douma had learned from the European immigrants that were her father's family, but only a tiny part of her own heritage), and in the middle it was pink and brownish and distended, very distended, not quite like anything that Anna Lee had ever imagined as part of the human body.

But as she watched, it opened further in the middle, and something new appeared—something round and slimy and shiny, the color of skin but an angry red, with fine black streaks on its surface.

The fine black streaks were hair. And this was it . . . the baby's head, at first just showing in a little circle as Anna Lee's mother's body parted for it, then pushing out further: big, bulging forehead, tiny ears on either side. Face up to Douma, who caught the underside of its head in one of her broad hands, and skillfully guided it out.

Anna Lee looked down at the baby's face, and for a moment, she thought that she saw its eyes open. The baby seemed to be looking back up at her, recognizing her, judging her.

She was never sure. Certainly not then. And even years later, when she understood that babies were always born with their eyes closed, and that it must have been some sort of illusion, some trick of the light or her imagination, she was still not sure. Because the image was too vivid: jet black eyes, open, looking up at her, seeming to know who she was and all about her.

The baby's arms were out now, and its trunk, and its legs, folded one over the other, then popping loose and waving as Douma held it under its bottom. At the base of its belly, there was a little nubbin of flesh, just like boy baby puppies had.

Douma raised the baby up by its heels and slapped it on the bottom, so that it yelped like a little puppy, and then began to cry, insistent, angry human cries.

There was a long, ropy thing, too, still connected to her mother's body. The baby was still attached to her mother . . . how could that be? Then Douma severed the ropy thing with her teeth, and the baby and mother were separate. Douma tied the part that was still attached to the baby in a little knot.

Anna Lee slipped out of the room, and went to sit by the fireplace in the store. The fire there was dancing too, more wildly and frantically than the one in the cabin because it had burned so low, and the flames were tiny and isolated from one another, just like frightened, lost children.

Anna Lee got another log, one that was small enough for her to carry. She threw it down on top of the fire, and jumped back as the sparks flew up. She got a poker, held it out at arm's length, and pushed the new log a little farther in. Slowly, it began to become part of the fire, and the fire kept on burning for her.

Douma took the baby, bathed it in warm ashes, and wiped it clean with moss, just as the Cree midwives had always done. She had made ready a chunk of hardened fat, with one end tapered into a nipple, as the Cree midwives had always done. She put it into the baby's mouth: he would suck on it until the next day, when Charlotte's milk would come in.

She wrapped the baby in a blanket, and put him in the moss bag that they had hung like a hammock next to Charlotte's bed. She left him there while she attended to the afterbirth, cleaned up, and got the mother comfortable. Then she picked the baby up again, and held him in her arms as she folded the coverlet back from his face and hands, and finally brought him down and placed him in the arms of his mother.

Charlotte had passed out for a moment, after the baby was out of her, but she regained consciousness quickly. Douma was holding the baby in front of her, and looking down into its tiny face.

Douma looked at the black, straight hair on the newborn's head, the hair that was to fall out soon after his birth, and be replaced in time by coppery hair like his mother's. She saw the dark, almond-shaped eyes, and the shape of the puckered, newborn mouth, and she knew that this was no English baby. No matter who the mother was, no matter who she claimed that the father might be, Douma recognized one of her own kind when she saw it. The baby was a *métis*.

She handed the tiny bundle to Charlotte.

"It's a boy," she said.

Charlotte cradled the baby, and looked down into his face. She smiled at him, and tickled him under the chin with her forefinger.

"He looks healthy," she said.

"Healthy all right," Douma said. "Fine baby. Big feet an' hands. Be big strong man when he grow up."

"Like his father," Charlotte said.

"Um." Douma gave her careful, noncommittal assent, as Charlotte continued to stare down at the baby nestled in her arms.

"We'll call you James," she said. "James Peter Graham, Jr."

"Good name," Douma said.

"His father's name," Charlotte said.

Little James opened his dark eyes again, and his mouth, and began crying.

* * *

Anna Lee got up from where she had been sitting before the fireplace, and went to look out the front window of the store. The rain had stopped by this time, and there was a three-quarter moon framed between two clouds, illuminating their edges so that it gave them bright, silvery linings.

"Anna Lee!" her mother called out to her from the next room. "Anna Lee! Come on in here now and see your little brother."

Anna Lee did not move right away. She stayed looking at the moon, and though she knew she was supposed to be happy, she wanted to cry. She was thinking about her father, and missing him.

"Anna Lee!"

She left the window reluctantly, and went back to look at the baby, whose face was buried against his mother's shoulder, so that Anna Lee could hardly see him anyway.

2

AT six years old, James Graham was already big and husky for his age. He was chubby and awkward in the way little boys become when they suddenly grow very large, but he was also surprisingly strong. He had grown tremendously over the period of one winter, from a toddler of five to a brawny boy.

It had made a big change in his personality, too. No more was he content to follow his older sister Anna Lee around. Now he had become aggressive, tyrannical, insistent on being the leader.

He took after his mother. Everyone said so. He had Charlotte's copper-colored hair, her squarish face, her thin mouth that could press into a wrinkled line of concentration whenever he wanted to think something through, or just to shut out the outside world.

In that summer, his mother was at her busiest, and had the least time for him. So it was Anna Lee's responsibility to mind him.

Charlotte worked in the garden out behind their cabin, or she was in the store, waiting on some customer or other. There were many more of them in the summertime, as the population of central Canada was on the move, breaking free from winter's restraints. The buffalo hunters were back on the prairie then. The trappers had broken their isolated winter camps, and were heading back in to civilization, with their bundles of pelts for sale. Some who were ready to settle down were on the move, looking for new ground to homestead, and others were just traveling to check up on relatives from whom they had been cut off over the long winter.

Anna Lee minded the store, too. She was eleven, now, and she did the cooking and cleaning. She kept the big stews and soups going on the kettle over the fireplace, and when Charlotte was out working in the garden or chopping wood for the woodpile, she would wait on customers. Standing on tiptoe, she would weigh out coffee or nails, count out bullets, and make change, stacking the coins up and counting them out so as to make sure that she got the figures right. She was not as good with numbers and arithmetic as her mother, who was forever studying numbers out of big schoolbooks, but she could make the right change if she worked at it.

Little James had almost nothing to do in the way of chores. He weeded in the garden alongside his mother, but that was all. And even there, he did not have to do a very good job. Charlotte would follow along behind him and pick the clumps of Timothy grass and ragged Queen Anne's lace that he had missed.

Anna Lee did not mind that she had to work, while James was almost totally excused from it. She was used to working; it was part of her. And he was the baby, after all.

She began to mind it a little more when he grew to less than a head shorter than she was.

It bothered her, as well, that he knew he was more privileged than she. He knew that she had to do her chores, while he could get away with doing nothing. He started acting like a little prince in front of her, and she felt like punching him sometimes, except that she knew that she would have to answer to her mother's wrath if she were ever to do any such thing.

But there was a good side to having a little prince in the family, too. James was allowed to wander off and play almost whenever he felt like it, which was something that she had never been allowed to do. It was her job to accompany him and make sure he was safe. So at those times, she got to go and play, too.

One day, early in July, James took it into his head to wander off, and Anna Lee went with him, leaving the bell at the entrance of the store so Charlotte could hear it from the garden if there were any customers. James wanted to go down by the lake, the small lake which was about half a mile from the cabin. They had never gone down there alone before.

James led the way, as always; trotting along in front of her for the entire half mile, a much longer distance than Anna Lee would have guessed that he could sustain. But somehow he made it, and then he threw himself down in a sulky heap on the grass by the lake's rim, and complained loudly.

"My feet hurt."

"Well, what do you want me to do about it?" Anna Lee said crossly.

I'll be hanged if I'm going to carry him home, Anna Lee thought. It's not my fault if his feet hurt. I don't care if I do get in trouble. And I don't care what Mama says.

She had a good idea that she might be in trouble already, anyway. She did not imagine that her mother would approve of their going down to the lake in the first place. She had never expressly forbidden them to, but Anna Lee knew that was only because it had never occurred to her that James could go that far.

It was a small lake, one of the little bodies of water that were sprinkled around the larger Lake Winnipeg. They could see across to the other side from where they sat. The other side was tree-lined backed up against the forest, and sometimes—Anna Lee remembered from walks down to the lake with her father years ago—one could see caribou or deer, possibly even a stately elk come out of the trees and lower its great antlered head down to take a drink from the dark water. Wolves came down, two at a time, the wolf and his mate who were together for life, so her father told her. Bears, big black bears who looked so funny and clumsy, but were the most dangerous animal in the woods, her father said. But way over on the other side of the lake, drinking or fishing with their big paws, they were no threat, and she loved to watch them.

Anna Lee liked the lake. It was so open on the one end, so closed on the other. One end practically a part of her own back yard, the other wilderness, mysterious and dangerous.

She had not been down to the lake since her father died, but in her mind she had come often, and alone. She pretended that she was alone now, and she looked across into the shadows of the trees on the other side, but no wild creatures showed themselves.

James had gotten bored with complaining, and was prowling along the bank of the lake, throwing sticks and stones to see them splash, walking down to the edge of the lapping water and then running back up the bank, away from it.

Anna Lee could hear the noises he was making, and she listened with one ear while she continued to gaze out over the lake, and think her own thoughts. Then he was quiet, and when the lack of noise sank into her consciousness, she began to worry.

He's all right, she told herself. Nothing could have happened. I would have heard a splash if he'd fallen in.

"James?" she called out in an irritated voice, in the direction she had last noticed him.

There was no answer.

Oh, that stupid . . . She got up from where she was sitting, and went down to see what sort of mischief he had managed to get himself involved in, and what she ought to be doing along the lines of scolding him and getting him out of it.

"Anna Lee! Anna Lee!" his voice reached her before she saw him, and his excited tone told her that at least he was alive and out of danger.

"Where are you?"

"Down here! Come and take a look at this?"

"Down where?" she called back, but she had gotten a fix on his voice, and she headed for it. "Take a look at what?" she yelled as she drew near.

She walked, ran, and slid down the steep embankment to the stretch of marshy sand at the lake's edge, and saw James standing next to a small rowboat, half on the sand, half in the water, and tethered to a tree stump.

"How about it, Anna Lee? Ain't it a beauty? What do you think?"

It was a real rowboat, one that might even have been bought in a store, not just an Indian canoe. But Anna Lee did not stop for long to scrutinize it. She took James by the hand and jerked him away from it.

"I think you're not getting in it, that's what I think," she told him.

"Yes, I am!" He pulled away from her, and ran back to the rowboat. "We're going to take a ride."

"No, we're not."

"Yes, we are."

"Mama wouldn't allow it."

"She's not here."

"It's dangerous."

"I don't care. I want to do it. I want to go for a boat ride."

Anna Lee hated being put in the position of the responsible one, the one whose job it always was to say no. She thought about the woods on the far side of the lake. And the boat was singing its siren song to her, too. She imagined what it would be like in the woods on the far side of the lake. She imagined what it would be like to row out to the middle of the lake, as near to one side as to the other, and just float there, rocking up and down on the surface of the water.

"Well, you can't," she said testily. "No boat ride, and that's final. Now come on back up to the field with me. We've got to get home, and I don't want you getting any more tired out so you'll nag me about how much your feet hurt all the way home. Come on. I don't want to have to tell you twice, or you're really going to be in for it."

Anna Lee turned around again and began to climb back up the embankment. She kept her back to James, but she stopped every few steps along the way and listened for some sound that would indicate that he was following her. She heard sounds, and she tried to translate them into the sounds of footsteps, but it was a hopeless cause. Finally, she had to turn around and check on him.

James had been busy. In just a few moments, he had managed to work the rope loose from where it had been looped around the treetrunk, and he was just tossing it into the rowboat.

"What do you think you're doing? You stop that this

instant! Put that rope back where you found it and get on up here!''

With a grimly willful expression on his face, James walked to the bow of the boat, and put his shoulder to it. He leaned hard against it, trying to dislodge the craft and push it out into the water.

''You'll never do it!'' Anna Lee shouted at him. But the tide was up, the boat's center of gravity was just barely on the sand, and a rising wave helped him out. The rowboat floated free in the lake, and James ran around and clambered over the side of it.

''Too late! Too late! You can't come! I'm going to go for a boat ride all by myself,'' he crowed at her triumphantly.

The boat bobbed up and down in the water, slipping a little farther away from shore with each lapping and receding wave.

''Oh, all right,'' Anna Lee said. ''I can't let you go out there all by yourself.''

''Too late! You can't catch me!''

In another couple of minutes it would be too late, unless she wanted to swim after him. She took off her shoes and stockings, and placed them up on the bank out of reach of the lapping waves.

''All right, here I come,'' she said.

3

"DO you have any oars?" she called out to him as she came up alongside the boat.

"I don't know."

"Stupid idiot! Take a look down on the bottom. By your feet!"

"Don't call me stupid."

By that time she had reched the boat herself and was climbing in over the side.

"It's all right," she said. "They're here. How stupid can you be—to go out in a boat without even knowing whether or not there are oars in it."

"I knew they were there all the time," James said petulantly.

"You are going to get yourself in such trouble someday," Anna Lee said, squeezing out the water from the hem of her skirts, which she had not succeeded in keeping from getting drenched.

"Am not."

Anna Lee picked up one oar, and stuck it in one of the oarlocks.

She had been in a rowboat before. Many years ago, when she was not even James's age. She had been with her father. She remembered it as she remembered other vignettes involving things she had done with her father, with incredible clarity of detail but without a context. She could not remember how old she had been, or why they had gone out in a rowboat, or whether her mother had been along—just his face smiling at her as she sat on the wide stern seat of the boat, and his big hands, and the oars in the oarlocks.

So she knew that you faced backwards when you rowed a boat. She was a little surprised at how heavy the oar was. They had seemed like matchsticks in her father's hands; she had not even thought of them in terms of physical effort.

But she got the oar in the lock, and tipped it so that the blade was up in the air, and the point of the shaft rested against the bottom of the boat. Then she went through the same procedure with the other oar.

But the boat was moving quiet well by itself, drifting along with the tide, and there was no need to row, Anna Lee was content to let it drift, while she looked over the side at the dark water slipping by, and the occasional silvery flashes of fish swimming just beneath the surface.

Charlotte left the garden when the sky began to grow dark, and headed up to the store. She found it empty, and went back outside to look around for the children. They were nowhere in sight.

"James!" she called out. "Anna Lee! Come back to the house this instant—there's a storm coming up."

No answer.

"Anna Lee! James! Where are you?"

She put on a slicker, and went out. Already the grass was tilted at an angle, and the leaves on the trees were turned over, their light undersides showing to the wind. The rain clouds had given a purple cast to the sky, and a muted tone to all the colors of field, woods, garden and house. The color was eerie now, almost glowing, but in a few minutes there would be no color at all: everything would be grey, seen through the lashing rain of a prairie cloudburst.

Some instinct led Charlotte's feet down toward the lake.

She walked slowly and tentatively at first, stopping every few yards to turn around in all directions, and call out the children's names over and over, with ever-increasing urgency. But as she continued on in the same direction, toward the lake, her instinct grew stronger and stronger and her pace grew faster, until finally she gave up stopping to call them and broke into a run, just as the heavens were split apart by a shaft of lightning and a crack of thunder, and a rain mixed with hailstones lashed down on the earth.

She took the embankment in three running, bounding steps, and reached the edge of a lake that was being whipped by the wind into waves that crested in foamy whitecaps, that was being battered by sheets of rain and hailstones the size of camphor balls.

And out on the lake, about fifteen or twenty yards from the shore, was a small frail rowboat, with her two children in it.

The rain had come up so suddenly, Anna Lee only saw it forming a few minutes before it struck. She sprang to the middle seat of the rowboat, and grabbed an oar in each hand, feeling their heaviness anew as she pushed them out toward the water, and tried to control them enough so that she could begin to stroke.

It was no use. The water was too heavy against them. She did not have a prayer of moving the oars through it, and she had to pull up the blades again and haul them back in before she lost them.

"Come on, row!" James said to her. "It's going to rain. Row us to shore."

Anna Lee felt tears of frustration welling up inside her. But she stifled them. She would not cry; she had a job to do. She had to get them to shore.

So she tried again, with one oar this time. She held it with both hands, let it down carefully into the water, not too deep, and pulled on it with all her might.

It worked, after a fashion. The oar pushed the water backwards, and the boat moved perceptibly. But it was only around, not forward: with one oar she could do no more than propel them in a circle.

"I wanna go home," James said, still peevish, not really aware enough of the danger they were in to be scared.

"If you want to go home, you're going to have to help me," Anna Lee told him.

"No. You do it. I'm too little."

"I can't do it alone. You'd better help, or we'll never get to shore. Now, come on. Sit up here next to me, and do what I tell you to."

She packed enough urgency and authority into her voice to make James stop complaining, at least for the moment, and to bring him up to take his place on the seat next to her.

"Now pick up the other oar—be careful, don't drop it—and hold it in your two hands like this." Anna Lee pushed her hands forward, wrapped around the oar, and showed him. He gripped his in the same way.

"It's heavy."

"I know it's heavy. Now dip it into the water very carefully, when I tell you to. Not too far—just get the blade barely under water. Then pull back on the handle of the oar when I tell you to. Got that?"

James nodded.

"All right . . . dip! And . . . pull!"

The boat moved forward. Just a little bit; but it was moving. Maybe they could make it work.

"Now . . . dip! And . . . pull!"

Again, a little progress.

"And . . . dip! And . . . pull!"

And the rain struck.

"Harder! Anna Lee shouted. "We have to do it harder. Dip! . . . And . . . pull!"

But the wind was up fiercely now, and the boat was no longer even responding to their attempts.

"Harder!" she said again fiercely. "You have to do it harder, or it won't work!"

"I don't care. I can't do it. I want to go home." James said, starting to sniffle. "I give up." And he put down the oar.

"Wait! Give me that! Anna Lee shrieked.

But it was too late. The oar slid out through the oarlock even as she lunged for it, and floated off out of reach, bobbing up and down across the hills and valleys made by the surging waves.

"Stupid!" Anna Lee yelled at him, and she hit him hard, on the side of his head.

That was the first thing Charlotte saw, when she reached the edge of the lake.

"Waaaa!" James wailed. "You hit me! I'm gonna tell Mama! I wanna go home!"

"Shut up! Shut up!" Anna Lee screamed at him over the sound of his howling, as it merged with the howling of the wind. She flailed away at the water with the one remaining oar, but now she was only slapping meaninglessly at the surface, while the boat went on drifting crazily, bobbing on the waves.

Charlotte was still standing on the bank, calling out to her children to come back to shore. There was no way that either of them could have heard the sound of her voice over the storm, but James looked up and caught sight of her waving.

"Mama! Mama!" he called to her. He jumped up and down and waved back at her frantically, with both arms flailing.

"*Don't!*"

But Anna Lee's warning was too late. And her desperate attempt to pull him back down was too late. The boat began to tip, and James lost his balance. Anna Lee grabbed his hand, but his feet slid out from under him, and he fell heavily. His head cracked against hers, and stunned her for a moment.

When she recovered her senses, he was in the water and the boat itself was tipping over, and she was being thrown out of it too.

She hit the water on her back, with her face up, and she looked up just in time to see the capsizing rowboat coming down on her.

It seemed just to hang in space, defying the laws of gravity. She had an idea that it would suspend itself there forever, if she wanted it to. She would have all the time in the world to swim leisurely backwards, out of its trajectory. If she could just do it . . . her mind was racing, but her body seemed to be in the same odd condition of suspended animation as the rowboat, and she could not move.

And suddenly there was no more time, and the boat was down on top of her.

She jerked her head backward, moving quickly at the last split second, but it hit her shoulder, a heavy, painful blow that numbed her whole arm so that she could no longer move it.

She paddled with the other, just trying to keep herself afloat. She looked around for James, but she could not find him.

The minute she saw James stand up in the boat, Charlotte had been galvanized out of her state of helpless spectatorship. She had her boots, her slicker, her full shirtwaist dress and petticoat off; she plunged into the foaming water in her shift and began swimming out toward the over turned craft.

Desperation lent power to her strokes, and she cut through the turbulent surface of the lake, straight toward the spot where James had fallen. She found him there, spluttering, flailing with his arms, just bobbing up to the surface but about to go under again, and she grabbed him with one strong forearm around his chest.

"Mama!" he opened his mouth to say, but a wave stopped the word in the middle, and he began choking again. It filled him with a new panic, and he struggled and kicked in Charlotte's arms.

She knew that she ought to knock him out, and carry him limp, but she just could not bring herself to hit him. All she could do was to tighten her grip, and get him over to the upside down rowboat, which was still floating nearby.

"Hold on!" she said, and hoisted him up to the length of both her arms, toward the top of the boat. His panic worked for them now, as he grabbed for the solid object, and flattened himself against it.

Charlotte herself was pushed under by the counter-thrust of getting James up onto the boat, and she swallowed water. She came up coughing, but she opened her eyes, tried fruitlessly to wipe them with one hand, and looked about for Anna Lee.

"Mama!"

She heard the cry faintly, and saw one thin arm slicing the air above the surface of the waves. She swam over.

"Can you swim?" she shouted to her.

"I can't move my arm."

"Grab hold of my neck with your good arm, then. And kick your feet."

Anna Lee did as she was told, paddling with her legs and feet to try to help pull her weight, as Charlotte brought her over to the rowboat.

There, Charlotte disengaged Anna Lee's arm from around her neck, and put it on the floating bow of the boat.

"Hold on tight," she said. "I'll be back."

She swam around to the side of the boat, and held up her hand to James.

"Come to Mama, dearest," she said. "I'll take you in to shore."

"No-o-ooo!" James screamed. He held tightly to the hull of the boat, his torso pressed flat against it, arms and legs spread-eagled around it, unwilling to budge an inch.

"Come on, James, come to Mama. It'll be all right. You'll be safe. I'll take you back to shore with me. Just let go, and I'll catch you."

"No-oo-oo!"

Charlotte reached up to grab the boy's leg. He kicked at her violently, in a complete state of panic and out of control. She kept on grabbing, he kept on kicking. Her little finger was bent back, the nail ripped. She experienced the pain sharply for a moment, but there was no time to think about it.

She put it out of her mind. She struck quickly, like a

snake, gripped James around his ankle, and pulled him off the top of the boat.

He hit the water thrashing, hysterical, clawing at her face and pulling her hair.

"James . . . James, baby, it's Mama, it's all right," Charlotte said, trying to shield her face both from him and from the waves. But nothing she said made any difference to his hysteria. And she knew that there was only one thing to do.

She clenched her hand into a fist, and hit him hard on the point of the jaw.

He relaxed, and she caught him under the armpits again, and started toward shore.

It seemed farther—twice as far, going back in, as it had coming out. The current felt stronger, and her body was weaker. But she clutched her son under her forearm, and kept swimming until her feet could touch the bottom, and she could walk in the rest of the way.

She laid him down high up on the beach, out of reach of the waves, and sank to her knees beside him. For a few seconds she hugged the ground, and then she pulled herself back up to her feet.

"Wait here, darling," she said. "Mama will be right back."

"Don't go, Mama!" James said, as he recovered consciousness. "Stay with me."

"I have to go get Anna Lee."

"No! I'm afraid!"

Charlotte was exhausted, spent. She did not think she could go back out there a second time. She did not even want to.

But she had to.

She took a deep breath, and plunged back into the icy, turbulent waves of the lake.

* * *

Jamie and Anna Lee sat side by side in front of the fireplace, wrapped up in blankets. Anna Lee's left arm was in a sling, holding up a homemade bandage and splint.

Charlotte went back to the stove, to get the water for the chamomile tea she was brewing for them.

And James turned to Anna Lee, and made a face at her.

"She saved me first," he said.

4

NOT long after that, Charlotte decided to move back into town. There was a dry goods emporium for sale in Fort Garry, and Charlotte bought it. She had the cash for the down payment—from Graham, from her own savings, no one knew for sure. The point was, she had it. And an afternoon spent with Morris Holbrook, the president of Fort Garry's bank, was enough to overcome his doubts about her, doubts that went a long way back to the time of her previous residence in Fort Garry, and to convince him that she was a good risk for a loan.

Finally, she had to win the approval of William Mactavish, the local governor of the Red River settlement for the Hudson's Bay Company; and after she had done that, the last obstacle to her securing a loan was removed. There was no force, not the government of the newly formed Confederation that had united all Canada east of the Rockies, nor the crown itself in England, that was as powerful in the Red River settlement as the Hudson's Bay Company.

* * *

The Company had been founded in 1670, as the first British stronghold in what was then New France. Two French adventurers, Groseillers and Radisson, were the first *coureurs de bois*, bush rangers, as the roving fur traders were called, to penetrate the dense woods and rich fur areas around Hudson's Bay, an area claimed in theory by the British because of the explorations of Henry Hudson, but of no special interest to them because of its remoteness and extreme difficulty of access.

Groseillers and Radisson made expeditions into the Upper Country in 1654 and again in 1660, bringing back incredibly rich cargoes of furs both times. They were welcomed as heroes by the French, who were badly feeling an economic pinch at that time, as many of the furs that were taken along the Great Lakes then were finding their way down to the British commercial center at Albany.

But the governor of New France, D'Argenson, got too greedy. He looked at the flow of soft, warm, luxuriant riches coming out of the Northwest, and decided to grab off as big a piece of it as he could. He told Groseillers and Radisson that if they wanted a license to trade out of Montreal, they would have to agree to take along two of his servants, and they would have to share half of their profits with him. The traders refused the deal, and went off into the interior without a license.

When they got back in 1663, D'Argenson was waiting for them. He had their furs impounded, and they ended up losing sixty per cent of all that they had made.

It was an expensive victory for D'Argenson, and even more expensive for New France. Groseillers and Radisson were Frenchmen, but they were businessmen first. They took their business to England, where Charles II, when he saw the kind of profits that could come rolling in from the fur trade, was glad to go along with them. In 1670, he chartered a company to trade into Hudson's Bay. His cousin, Prince Rupert, was put at its head, and the new organization was granted the monopoly of trade in that area, and full ownership of all lands that were watered by rivers that led into Hudson's Bay.

So English commerce became a part of French Canada's life; and there was nothing that could be done about it, although the French tried. Intermittent small wars were waged over the right to the land for the next few decades, until the Treaty of Utrecht that ended the War of Spanish Succession, or Queen Anne's War as it was called in the New World, in which France officially ceded all of the contested territory to the Hudson's Bay Company.

A century after Groseillers and Radisson entered the Upper Country, in September of 1759, the British general James Wolfe defeated the Marquis de Montcalm's forces in battle on the Plains of Abraham, outside Quebec, and all of Canada was England's, if she wanted it.

Actually, England was not at all sure that she did. During the peace negotiations that followed, at the conclusion of the Seven Years' War in Europe, England tried to give Canada back to France and take the sugar-bearing island of Guadaloupe instead. But the French were tired of the financial and military drain that Canada had become for them. England had won it; England could have it.

So by the treaty of Paris in 1763, Canada became a British colony. And the chief British mercantile organization in Canada was the Hudson's Bay Company.

And a hundred years after that, by the mid-19th century, the Hudson's Bay Company owned Western Canada. It had eliminated or absorbed any rival fur-trading operations.

And while the territorial rights of the Dominion government in Ottawa to the area west of the Great Lakes were fuzzy, the rights of the Hudson's Bay Company were quite clear: a charter from the Crown, giving it full ownership of all the lands drained by the rivers flowing into Hudson's Bay.

If the Company seemed to own the land by deed, they certainly controlled it in fact. There was no one else. The only law and order that was provided west of the Great Lakes was that which was provided by the Hudson's Bay Company.

That meant that there was really nobody but the Company to set the borders of their empire, either. And as far as they were concerned, those borders stretched to include the valleys of the Saskatchewan River and the Red River, although neither of them flowed into the bay.

And certainly included was the Red River settlement.

So when Charlotte Graham convinced William Mactavish that she could take care of the company's interests in Fort Garry, she became a blue-chip investment for any bank.

She bought a house in Fort Garry, and put her children in school. Anna Lee knew how to read and write and do numbers. Her mother had taught her, and she was beginning to try and teach James, too, in that last autumn by the Winnipeg River, but as yet he had shown neither the interest nor the patience to learn.

But he was still a baby. He would learn his letters and figures in time from the schoolmaster, learn as much as he had to. This was still the frontier, after all, and there were other skills besides book learning that mattered on the frontier.

Charlotte made a few mistakes that first year in Fort Garry. She tried to run the business the way she had run her own little store in the backwoods. She took too much on herself, assuming that she and Anna Lee could do everything, just as they had done it before.

But she learned quickly. She hired help. She learned how to fire people, how to judge an employee's effectiveness, how to delegate responsibility. She expanded the business. She learned, also, what it was like not to be her own boss. She reported to the Hudson's Bay Company, and she gave them what they wanted. Mactavish was very pleased with her.

Douma came to call. She was older, and frail. She no longer practiced as a midwife. Charlotte greeted her politely but not warmly. She did invite her to stay for dinner. Douma declined, but said that she would wait to see the children when they came home from school.

Anna Lee remembered Douma very well. James, of course, did not remember her at all. When he was told that she was the woman who had delivered him, he responded with a sullen shyness. He ducked his face down when she bent to kiss him, and permitted himself to be kissed only on the top of his head.

Anna Lee felt a surge of warmth and comradeship for the old woman. She hugged her, and stood close to her, while James retreated to a safe and formal distance, and waited with ill-disguised impatience to be allowed to leave the room.

But James was the one whom Douma scrutinized most carefully. She appraised the coppery hair, the square jaw, the thin lips, and all the rest.

"Looks just like me, doesn't he?" Charlotte said. "Spittin' image."

"Jus' lak you," Douma replied.

Anna Lee wanted Douma to stay longer. She felt she

would have liked to ask the old woman questions. She felt that there were mysteries that Douma could explain to her, but she was not sure what they were, and she would not have known how to ask.

But Douma would not stay, anyway. She said her farewells and left, hobbling slowly on feet that hurt her and legs that were no longer interested in carrying her where she wanted to go.

A month later, Charlotte heard that Douma was dead. She found that she was not particularly sorry to hear the news.

Another month or so after that, James arrived home from school with his nose bleeding, his cheek scraped, and a rent in the knee of his trousers.

"James! What happened?" his mother exclaimed when she saw him.

"Nothin'."

"What do you mean, nothing? You have been fighting?" She tried to grab him and look at him, but he shied away from her.

"I got into a fight, yeah."

"Well, I don't want you to do it again," Charlotte said sternly. "It's a terribly naughty thing to do. Now go and get yourself cleaned up, and give Anna Lee those trousers to mend. Are you hurt?"

"Nah, I'm all right. The other kid, he's the one who's hurt."

"Well, go and wash up, then. What was it about?"

"Nothin'."

His eyes grew very evasive, and he backed off a couple more steps, then turned around and started to walk away from her.

"Nothing?" she asked sharply.

"Nothin'."

He walked off toward the washstand. But half a dozen steps later, he whirled around to face Charlotte, and there were tears in his eyes.

"He said that I was a bastard, that Papa wasn't my real papa. He said my real papa was some kind of an Indian. That's not true, is it?"

5

THE Red River settlement was founded in 1811 by Thomas Douglas, Earl of Selkirk, a Scottish philanthropist who had attempted to find a place in the New World for the influx of Scottish settlers at the end of the 18th century, mostly crofters, tenant farmers who had been driven off their land by crop failure and landlord foreclosure.

Lord Selkirk's first Scottish colony was on Prince Edward Island, in 1803. Then he moved on to the Western plains, where he planned to buy 116,000 square miles of land in the Red River valley, and start his next colony.

The Hudson's Bay Company was not pleased, at first. They did not like the idea of settlers anywhere in western Canada. As they reasoned it, the more settlers, the less wilderness land and the fewer fur-bearing animals. But there was a need for some source of food and provisions for the fur traders, too; and the Company, after some negotiations with Selkirk, worked out a deal. Selkirk invested heavily in the Hudson's Bay Company, soon sat on its board of directors, and was permitted to buy his 116,000 acres and move in his colony of Scottish farmers.

By 1834, Selkirk was dead, and his heirs sold the land back to the Company. The population then was made up of the Scottish settlers, and the *métis* majority. The *métis* were both French- and English-speaking, the descendants of the original fur traders and their Indian brides. There had been only one white woman in the Northwest country before the Scots came in, and marriage between whites and Indians had been the rule rather than the exception, a custom which had led to peaceful coexistence between the Indians and the fur traders.

The whites and the *métis* coexisted easily too, for the most part. There was some strain. The *métis* thought of the 'gardeners,' as they called the farm-bound Scots, as stiff and unyielding, and the Scots looked at the *métis* as irresponsible, if not immoral, for their more freewheeling life style. But they were all Westerners, all part of a pioneer community that had its own values, and its own culture.

It was a culture that was to be threatened in another three decades, with an influx of new settlers from Canada and the United States, with an ugly new sentiment of racisim that took the *métis* as its target, and by Canada's new expansionist policies. But the balance was still there in 1843, when Charlotte Sayles arrived in Fort Garry.

She had moved across the border from Minnesota in 1843, and drifted up northward to the Red River settlement, driven by a restlessness inside her that she did not want, but could not ignore. She had been the second youngest of five children on a farm family in Wayzata, just outside of the prairie town and trading post of St. Paul. She had been the first girl, the one who kept house. She left home when she was sixteen, without telling her parents, or anyone except her little ten-year-old sister, whom she had successfully terrorized into not revealing her whereabouts to anyone until Charlotte was far enough away from home that she could not be caught and brought back.

She got a job as a waitress in Fort Garry, and lived in a rooming house. She was looking for a husband on the Canadian frontier, and she had arrived at the right time, just when white women were becoming a valuable commodity in the settlement. She got two offers in the first week, one from a homesteader and the other from a storekeeper in Kildonan, but she turned them both down without really understanding why.

And there were more offers in the next couple of years, while she went on working as a waitress in Fort Garry and sleeping alone, but she went on turning them down. She had changed her ambitions, it seemed, without even thinking about it. So she began to think about it. She was eighteen now, and it was time to decide what she really wanted to do with the rest of her life.

She could read and write, and she was ambitious. She got some books from the local schoolteacher, and began to teach herself figures and accounting. She had determined that she was going to make something of herself, and learning about numbers and business seemed like a good way to begin. She began to save a little money. She continued working as a waitress during the day, and five nights a week, she studied her books.

The other two nights, she worked at augmenting her savings. She had become a prostitute.

She lost her virginity that way, to a man who paid her. Afterwards, she could never remember him.

The hardest part of it was being both a citizen of the town of Fort Garry and being a prostitute. The other girls who worked at Mrs. Harris's house lived there, and almost never left it. Charlotte came and went, and she was not one of them.

She missed out on the companionship and solidarity they had with each other, and she was never allowed to forget, as she went about the rest of her life in Fort Garry, that she was beyond the pale of decent society. Always there were the turning of heads, the whispers, the overly familiar grins and hands from the customers at the restaurant, especially from those who had been her customers at Mrs. Harris's.

In the evenings, the other evenings, she had her books and her numbers, and the idea that she was going to make something of her life, somehow, if she went on studying.

But she was getting discouraged. The work at the restaurant was getting harder and harder to balance with the work at Mrs. Harris's. And she was afraid that her landlady was going to tell her to move out of her rooming house. She had just about decided to move into the whorehouse full time. She could study her numbers there, just as well as anyplace else.

And then, as suddenly, she changed her life again, on an afternoon when a man named Jim Graham walked into the restaurant.

He stared at her as he took her order, his eyes growing wider with a kind of recognition that was familiar enough to Charlotte. It meant that he had probably been lying on top of her at some time or other, over the past couple of nights.

But there was something different about Graham. For one thing, he did not say anything rude to her, or run his hand across her rump when she brought him his meal of black bread and rabbit stew.

Still, he kept on staring at her.

After a while, she began to search her memory for him; and she remembered that yes, he had been one of them.

But she could not remember anything more than that. One of them—nothing unusual, nothing special.

And still he kept looking at her, and lingering on in the restaurant. At first it made her uncomfortable, but then the discomfort passed.

There was nothing to fear from him, that seemed clear. No, the look he was giving her was appreciative—something that she was hardly used to these days in Fort Garry, since men had stopped proposing to her.

Well, she could not remember what being with him had been like, one way or the other, but then, she never could. It must have been pretty good for him, she decided.

But she knew that there was more going on in his mind than just that.

He spent a long time over his meal. He ordered coffee, and sat with it until it had grown cold, half of it still untouched in the cup. And after he left, she knew that he was waiting outside for her. She saw him out of the corner of her eye through the window a few times. Once or twice, their eyes even met, but she broke the contact very quickly, and went back to what she was doing.

At the end of her shift, she knew that he was still out there someplace. Jules, the owner of the restaurant, a brawny French-speaking *métis*, knew it too.

"You wan me to go out dere wit you?" he asked.

"No I don't think you'll have to, Jules," Charlotte told him.

"Lissen, *cherie*, you doan know what dat feller's up to, *hein*? You better . . ."

"I think I know what he's up to," she said.

She took off her apron and put on her heavy coat, and went out into the street. She turned, as she went out the door, in the direction she thought he was waiting. She walked down the board sidewalk, saw him out of the corner of her eye, and kept walking, toward him, past him, without acknowledging his presence. He put out a large hand and caught her arm.

She stopped, and faced him. She was not going to say anything until he did, and she waited for him to find words. It took a few minutes.

"I run a trap line up by the Winnipeg River," he said in a husky voice. "It's a good territory, still, if you know where to plant your traps. And I do."

"I'm sure you do," she said.

"I'm looking for a wife to go back up there with me."

"I'll go with you."

6

CHARLOTTE and Jim Graham built a cabin on the edge of the woods, South of Lake Winnipeg. It was close enough to the area where Jim ran his trap lines that he could use it as home base, and far enough away so that it did not bring the encroachment of civilization down on top of them.

Their home was in a sparsely traveled area, but on a trail that would be used by *coureurs de bois*, hunters, fur traders, and whatever other kind of traveler might pass through the area. It was a good location for Charlotte, who had determined to start a store of her own. She was not entirely satisfied that this was what she had done all her studying of mathematics for, but she was satisfied enough.

The store was not strictly legal, in that it was not chartered by the Hudson's Bay Company. Neither, for that matter, was Jim Graham's trap line. In fact, it was precisely fear of men like Graham that had been one of the Hudson's Bay Company's prime reasons for not encouraging population growth in the Red River area—independent trappers and fur traders, operating their lines in competition with the Company's monopoly.

The district marshal, an English-speaking *métis* named Jack Murphy, was responsible for the law in that area. Like all law enforcement officials in Red River, he was employed by the company. He knew about Jim Graham, but he had never been able to catch him with any evidence.

Charlotte Graham would have been a much easier target for Murphy's persecution, so she had to figure out a way to deal with him as part of her plan for setting up the store. She solved the problem in a way that she could manage, and in a way that satisfied Murphy: her sexual favors in return for his unspoken agreement to look the other way when it came to policing the Grahams' activities.

Jim Graham knew about the arrangement, and he did not object. He was not generally so sanguine; he was a jealous man, and he had made that clear from the outset, but he accepted Murphy as just another necessary fact of his life.

He knew, as well, that there would be no one else. Charlotte had not married him and moved out to a cabin in the woods in order to continue the life she had been leading at Fort Garry. She was through with all that, as through as could be. For anyone who asked, there was a firm, cold, and hostile response, with enough finality so that no one ever asked a second time. And for anyone who tried to insist, there was the rifle on the wall, and a lead-weighted club within easy reach, just under the counter.

Murphy was thrown from his horse in the spring of 1848, when the animal shied at a snake that was sunning itself on the trail. His foot caught in a stirrup, and he was dragged by the panicky horse for a quarter of a mile before his head hit a rock and his skull split wide open.

Charlotte was sorry to hear about Jack Murphy, but not

very sorry. She had grown used to having him in her life, and even fond of him in a way. He was part of her routine, brought her news from the outside world, and made very few demands—only one demand, really—on her. But it was relief to have him out of it.

At the same time, the Company's pressure on the independent trappers and trader in the area was easing up. One of their number, a French-speaking *métis* named Sayer, was arrested for trading without a license, and his pelts were confiscated.

A *métis* leader, a miller named Louis Riel, led an assortment of French and English-speaking *métis*, armed with rifles and pitchforks, to Fort Garry, where they surrounded the courtroom and would not let Sayer be brought in for trial until their demands were met: a fair jury selection for his trial, made up of his peers; a bilingual judge or at least a court-appointed interpreter, so that the defendant would know what was going on in the courtroom; and a defense attorney of his choice to represent him.

The demands were modest and reasonable enough, but they were symbolic, too, and the point was made. The Company realized it had to accede to them or face real trouble. And for all practical purposes, the battle was over. The Company had to deal with the pressure of the independents, and that meant that Louis Riel and his group had won freedom of commerce for every independent trapper and trader of the Red River settlement.

Charlotte settled down to the life of being a storekeeper, and Jim Graham's wife, and nothing more. If she had a past at all, she never alluded to it, nor did she ever recognize any allusions to it. And in a very short time, there were no allusions to it. A past is quickly forgotten on the frontier.

Life with Jim Graham meant life alone, a great deal of the time. The two of them were only together for short stretches. Then he would be gone again, for three or four months, following his trap lines.

When he was at home, they spent almost all of their time together. He repaired things in the house or the store, or he chopped and stacked wood in the woodshed next to the back door, where he could holler out to her; or he just sat in the store and whittled and watched her wait on customers.

Sometimes in the evening, in the warm months, they would get out of the store together, go and sit on a hillside, and watch the path of the setting sun down over the trees.

Every night that he was at home, they made love. Before Jim, Charlotte had never known the experience of making love with just one man, and now she learned about it, and grew to understand it. It required less guesswork, less in the way of quick reactions. It was more taking time, understanding, fitting her rhythms with his so that it became natural, comfortable, second nature.

While he was gone, she spent her evenings studying her books, and later, after Anna Lee was born, with the baby. She missed him when he left, but after he was gone, she was able to settle quite quickly and contentedly into the routine of being alone.

She never knew exactly how long he was going to be gone. But each time he returned, she would begin to sense it two or three days before he was actually there. It would start with a kind of tingling, an anticipation that she first felt as a point somewhere inside her, and that gradually built and spread through her during the day, as she went about her routine. Then her step would become a little lighter, her normally reserved personality a little warmer.

At night, the feeling would be even stronger, and as she lay in bed, all the feelings that had coursed through her all day would come together in a point once again, a point in between her legs, until she had to put her hand down there and rub to satisfy it, before she could go to sleep.

Over the next day or two it would grow and grow in intensity, flowing through her by day and focusing on that one tingling spot by night, until it reached a peak where both things were happening at the same time, and then—she could predict it almost to the minute—the door would open, Jim Graham would come lumbering in, and she would throw herself into his arms.

It was August, 1855. The weather was humid and steamy, even late into the evening. Some nights that summer, it had seemed that the sun would never set; it hung in the sky like a heart, and its glow lingered on long after its last rays had disappeared.

On one of those nights, Graham had wanted to make love to her on the hillside, in the tall grass and clover. She had let him, but not until she had made him chase her up hill and down, laughing and calling her name, until he finally got a big hand around her waist, and wrestled her to the ground.

"Don't you think we're getting too old for this kind of nonsense?" he asked, panting from the exertion and unbuttoning the front of her dress.

"Don't you think we're getting too old for *this* kind of nonsense?" she countered, raising her hips as she lay beneath him.

"No," he said.

"Neither do I."

He left the next morning, kissing her goodbye and squeezing her buttocks in the doorway. She watched him disappear into the forest, and then went back to her usual routine. By noon, she was once again used to being alone, and feeling comfortable with it.

The next day, though, she started to feel the tingle that

she normally felt only when Jim Graham was nearing home. But it was different this time, and she knew it was not right.

Disturbing, where other times it had always been exciting. And at night it was worse. An eerie, itchy feeling between her thighs. The next day was just as bad, and the night was worse. She could not sleep at all. Her body was completely out of kilter. The itching had become a burning, hot and unbearable.

Four-year-old Anna Lee watched her from a distance the next morning, instead of following around at her heels the way she normally did. Charlotte had not told her to stay away; Anna Lee seemed rather to be instinctively responding to a visible torment that had to be respected, and not approached too closely.

And late that morning, just as it had always done before, the feeling reached a peak. Just like the peak that told her Graham was home, but awful, painful. And this time . . .

She felt herself impelled to the door. It did not open for her, so she pushed it open from the inside, and stepped out in front of the store. And down the trail, coming slowly out of the forest, she saw a buckskin horse and a rider.

Not the right horse—not Graham's roan; and not Graham. It was Johnny Cederque, at *métis* trader and a friend of Graham's. Looking behind him, Charlotte saw that he was leading another horse, a roan. It appeared to be a pack horse.

But not a pack horse. It was Jim Graham's roan saddle horse, but there was no rider on it. Just something wrapped up in a blanket, and laid across the saddle, flopping down on each side.

"Was he dragged, Johnny?" Charlotte wanted to know. Her eyes were dry and glittering, and her body quivered with such a fine tremor that it was almost undetectable. "Like . . .?"

"Like the marshal?" Johnny said. "Nah, nothing like that. He was killed instantly, that's certain. Hit his head on a rock. I guess we can be grateful for that much, at least."

"I guess we can."

They buried him that same afternoon, in a clearing surrounded by a grove of poplars behind the store. Tiger roses bloomed there in the summer, and wild roses and sweet peas and morning glories and augur flowers. Johnny Cederque dug the grave, deep and narrow. Charlotte prepared the body for burial, and sewed the heavy shroud that they would bury him in. Anna Lee stood and watched Johnny from the edge of the grove.

They laid Jim Graham to rest there, and shoveled dirt over him. When the dirt on the grave was at a level with the ground around it, and sods had been tramped back into place, and a wooden cross had been pounded into the ground at the head of the grave, Johnny Cederque continued on his way, leaving Charlotte and her daughter alone.

Charlotte lay awake all that night, too. She did not feel as though she would ever sleep again. Her body was rigid, and her eyes were fixed wide open, staring at the darkness. Her own hands felt like talons to her. She could have clawed through the wooden bedstead, or turned them on herself and clawed her eyes out.

She arose at dawn, went out and drew water from the well. She found that she was looking over her shoulder as she walked, and she realized it meant that she was still looking down the trail, as though she still expected him to come home.

Worse, she could not break the habit. She kept doing it all day—stopping in the doorway and gazing down the trail, looking up expectantly whenever the door opened and someone new came into the store.

The release that always followed the tension that built up to his arrival had not come this time. The feverish nervousness just hung on. There was no longer anything for it to build up to, not with Jim Graham dead. Would it just build forever?

What would she do when it became intolerable? It had already become intolerable. And she was doing nothing about it; there was nothing to do. Nothing but tending the store, and lying awake at night, with her hands outside of the blankets, her fingers curved stiffly into unyielding talons.

Late the next afternoon, she began to hear a noise: a droning, ceaseless squealing sound far off in the distance. It was a commonplace enough sound on the prairie: a Red River cart, the indigenous two-wheeled vehicle of the plains. It was built all of wood—wooden fittings, wooden joints, wooden pegs to hold it together, an unpeeled poplar log for an axle. No grease was ever used on the axles of the Red River cart, on the theory that the fine grit and dust of the prairie would be absorbed into the grease, making it coagulate and cementing the wheels to the axles. So there was a constant screech as the car rolled along, like the sound of thousands of fingernails being drawn across a schoolroom slate.

Everyone who lived out on the plains got used to the sound of the Red River cart. It carried over the open prairies; it could be heard for miles and miles. The carts and their droning squeal passed by Charlotte's store several times a week, and they never drew so much as the lifting of an eyebrow from her.

But this one was different, somehow. The screech seemed to be vibrating in the air at the same pitch as her taut nerves. It stayed in her consciousness, keying her up more and more as it grew closer, until it stopped right outside the store. Then there was silence for a minute or so, a tense silence for Charlotte.

The door opened and closed behind a tall, broad-shouldered man, and Charlotted gasped in spite of herself at the sight of him.

"Hey, what is it, madame?" asked the stranger, in a big, booming voice. "You look lak you see beeg, scary ghost walk in. Mebbe you t'ink you know me from someplace, *hein*?"

"No," Charlotte said stiffly.

Charlotte was perplexed. This man looked nothing at all like Jim Graham. She could not imagine why she had reacted so strongly.

"No," she said, "that's not it at all. I was thinking of something else. I was just startled for a moment—it had nothing to do with you, I can assure you. Nothing at all."

"Hey, I doan mean to startle you," the stranger said. "I jus' come in to rest my bones, get a bite of stew, *n'est-ce pas*? My name ees Marotte."

"What can I do for you then, Mr. Marotte? You'd like some stew?"

"*Comment t'appelle toi?*"

"Mrs. Graham."

"Ah, Mrs. Graham! Nice English name. Me, I'm *métis*. *Bois-brulé*. You have a *nom chretieh* too, Mrs. Graham? A firs' name?"

"Charlotte."

"Charlotte, I lak dat. I have a firs' name too, is Gilles."

Charlotte pursed her lips, and nodded. Gilles Marotte was dressed in the *métis* style, gaily and colorfully, with fringed buckskin trousers, beaded moccasins, and a gaily colored sash around his waist. His hair was long, dark, and tangled, and his eyes glowed and sparkled under bushy eyebrows.

"What can I do for you, Mr. Marotte?" Charlotte repeated the question.

"You can t'ink about me again, nex' time someone comes in ze door an' you get dat special look in your eyes lak you know him, when you don't."

"I'm afraid I can't do that."

But he had made her smile, and they both knew it. He was still looking at her directly and frankly; and finally, she had to meet his eyes. He grinned at her, lifting one corner of his mouth to make his face lopsided, and she had to smile again.

Anna Lee had come out into the store, and she saw her mother smiling. She looked up at the man her mother had smiled at, and the man cocked his shaggy head to one side, made the lopsided face for her too, and waved at her.

"Hey, *ma petite*," he said to her. "*Comment allez-vous?*"

"Fine," Anna Lee said, and went on watching him with solemn eyes.

"I tak a bowl of stew an' a *biere*," Marotte said to Charlotte. "An' how about you? You have one wit' me, *hein?*"

"I only serve the customers, I never eat with them," Charlotte said. "Anna Lee, it's your bedtime. You get out of here and go to bed."

"All right, Mama."

"Good night, Anna Lee." Charlotte kissed her on top of her head, then turned her around by the shoulders so that she was facing the door.

"Good night, Mama."

"Hey, good night, *ma petite*," Marotte said. Anna Lee marched out of the room, and Charlotte went to get her customer the stew.

In the kitchen, she shivered, and for several minutes,

she could not stop shivering. What could she do when the feeling became intolerable? It had been intolerable.

But not like this. The pressure was even greater, now. She had to do something to relieve it.

She set the stew down in front of Marotte. He put his hand over hers.

"Hey, you Charlotte. You come sit down with Gilles, have dinner wit' me, *hein?* You look lak you need some rest."

His hand burned against hers, but it stopped hers from trembling.

"Come on, Charlotte. What do you say?"

"All right. I'll have a beer with you. I don't want—I don't think I could eat anything. Let me go out and get the beer, and I'll be right back."

"I wait."

As she picked the beer bottles up, her hands were trembling more than ever.

She never saw Gilles Marotte again. He left the next morning, and sometimes she thought she had dreamt him.

But the tight, oppressive feeling inside her was gone, too, and it did not come back. She cried for Graham the next night, and then she settled into the routine of life without him.

She ran the store alone, and when she discovered that she was pregnant, she made arrangements for the midwife, and kept on working. She kept her life, and her feelings, all to herself. And nobody, then or later, ever asked her any questions about the boy's father, though some were to speculate behind her back.

And she never had sex again with a man, after that night.

* * *

"He said I was a bastard, that Papa wasn't my real papa," James said to her. "He said that my real father was some kind of an Indian. That's not true, is it?"

Charlotte looked straight at him.

"It's not true," she said. "Your father was James Peter Graham, just like you are. And don't ever let anyone tell you differently."

7

MOVING back to Fort Garry was harder on Charlotte's children, in many ways, than it was on her. Certainly, it was harder on them than she had imagined it would be when she made the move.

For herself, there was no problem, and there would be none. That had been clear from the first day when she conferred with Morris Holbrook, the president of the bank, and not the slightest allusion was made to the fact that he had ever paid for her favors.

Charlotte's defense was an exterior so formidable that no one would have presumed to confront her with anything, or treat her with anything less than respect. But that same defense proved equally effective against her children. She was in many ways a loving and responsible mother. But when it came to dealing with whispers and half-understood rumors about their mother, Anna Lee and James were on their own.

James had more than one fight in school on the subject

of his parentage. There were several violent brawls, until the other boys realized that he was going to win, and win decisively, every time. James was big and strong, and he did not hold back anything in a fight. In fact, getting the upper hand seemed to inflame him all the more; and even when he was seven or eight, he sometimes had to be pulled off another boy before he could do him a really serious bodily injury.

It was always the same fight for James: the allusions to his ancestry. That was a strange business: the great majority of Red River settlers were *métis*. The early fur traders had all been single men, and many of them had married Indian women. The immigration of any white women at all was a recent phenomenon—but still, a racial consciousness had begun to show itself in the settlement.

As for Charlotte Graham's scarlet past, the little boys at Red River Academy were too young to understand what that meant. And by the time they got old enough, they were too afraid of James.

Anna Lee, at the Red River Academy for girls, heard some of those whispers.

There was no question of Anna Lee's parentage. She had hair the color of burnished copper, and a turned-up nose with a handful of freckles scattered across it. She had a long-legged, lithe but robust figure that would have been at home leaping a Highland brook or dancing through the heather on the hills.

She was exotic beauty in a land where the reason they had a girls' academy at all, in a country where education of females was of no more value than nipples on a stallion, was to separate the daughters of white men and *métis* women from their mothers, and teach them the Victorian graces and Victorian values.

Anna Lee, with her clear, pale complexion, was held up

as a model to the other girls, and she conducted herself accordingly. She was not sure that she had a right not to. But she was not so sure that she felt like a model. She sensed that there was another side to her; and when she heard the whispers about what her mother might have been—all couched in veiled, extremely indirect language—she began to wonder about her mother, and about herself.

At seventeen, and still unmarried, she went to work in her mother's store. Fort Garry was now Winnipeg, a thriving, growing plains town that had developed around the fort. It had a downtown business district, with a gun shop, a harness shop, a butcher shop, and a carriage shop prominent on Main Street. Charlotte Graham's general store occupied a central location, as did the bank. There were two hotels, Mrs. Harris's house was still there, on a side street, and there were three saloons.

The population of the Red River settlement in the mid-1860s was a little over 11,000, of which close to 10,000 were *métis*, equally divided between French- and English-speaking, and only about 1,500 white. It was still a population in which men far exceeded women, and in which white women of unmixed blood were the rarest of all. Anna Lee would have been special even if she had not been beautiful. But she was, and by seventeen she was fully developed, with round, full breasts that arced out from her body in breathtaking defiance of gravity.

She was a pearl of great price; and if she did not know it herself, she had her mother to tell her so, and her mother to remind her that such a pearl was not to be bestowed on any but the most worthy purchaser.

"You'll marry the right man," Charlotte told her. "And you'll make something of yourself. You're not going to be stuck in Winnipeg for the rest of your life."

"What's wrong with Winnipeg?" Anna Lee would retort.

Or, alternately, "What makes you think the right man is ever going to come to Winnipeg?"

But she had a feeling that, whatever she said, her life was going to turn out exactly the way her mother said it would. Something in her dreaded the prospect, even though she was not sure why. Surely, there could be nothing so terribly wrong with finding the right man.

She could do it, too—she, perhaps alone of the girls at the Red River Academy, alone of the girls in the settlement. She could be like Governor Mactavish's daughters, who wore beautiful clothes with lace trim and soft, shiny velvet collars.

She had only met Governor Mactavish's daughters a couple of times. They had been soft-skinned, and seemed impossibly fine for the border country. They had been sent to school back in Canada, to go to balls and soirees and cotillions, and meet proper young men to marry.

Sometimes, when she closed her eyes, Anna Lee imagined herself meeting her Prince Charming: handsome and rich, dashing and poetic. He would fall in love with her and take her to live with him in a fine house, with velvet curtains and linen table clothes and silver rings around the damask napkins.

In Canada. In Ottawa, or Montreal, or Quebec. Not in this primitive country which was no country except the Red River settlement.

Could she really find such a man? Not among the settlers of the Red River, that was for sure. Perhaps among the newcomers—the Canadians who were starting to cross the border from Canada and make their homes in Winnipeg and Kildonan, St. Boniface and Portage du Prairie, the ones who brought stories of what the ladies were wearing in Montreal, and who wanted to see the Red River settlement annexed by the Canadian government.

One such newcomer was Dr. John Schultz, who had

come out to Red River to practice as a physician, but who had quickly given that up to devote full time to business. He was her mother's partner, now. He had bought a half-interest in the general store for what Anna Lee gathered was a handsome figure, and he was now also advertising himself as being in the real estate business, though there scarcely seemed much call for a realtor in Red River, as things stood.

Dr. Schultz was a tall, forbidding man in his late twenties. He was an impeccable dresser, but coarse-featured, with a wiry beard that was full in the mustache and around the chin, closer-cropped around the sides of his face. He had a harsh voice and a harsh, appraising stare. He smiled seldomly, and when he did, it was often not a pleasant smile, and it was easy to wish that he had not bothered to essay it at all.

Schultz was the leader of the newly formed Canada First Party, the group that was trying to bring the Red River settlement into Canada. Anna Lee supposed that her mother was for it, too, since she was Schultz's partner. She knew that other people in the settlement were against it. She did not know how she felt about it herself—she did not think of it much one way or another, except when she heard other people talking about it in the store. It was hard to imagine Red River being a part of Canada. On the other hand, it might mean that she would finally get to meet that handsome Canadian who would sweep her off her feet and take her away.

She certainly hoped that he would not look anything like Dr. Schultz. But there had to be other Canadian men.

He had a friend, a Mr. Henry Sleight, who was coming out to join him in Winnipeg. Anna Lee had heard him talking about Henry Sleight and what she heard piqued her interest. Sleight was an English-born poet, quite well thought of in Canadian literary circles. But he was ambitious, too—Dr. Schultz predicted that once Sleight got to Red River, he would make a fortune in no time. He was reputed to be handsome, as well.

Anna Lee was not sure how handsome she thought he was, when she finally met him. He was blond, with a sandy-blond mustache. He was just a little plump, in the way that city people tend to be plump; but he was a tall, vigorous man, and the plumpness was not unattractive on him, except that it added a certain unformed look to him, as if he had not yet decided the sort of person he wanted to be. His eyes were heavy-lidded but alert, and a very light blue. He wore tweed suits, and spoke with a cultured accent. Certainly, most of the girls in the settlement thought he was handsome enough to have stepped out of a dream. And in certain ways, he was. Anna Lee was not altogether sure what her reservations about him were . . .

And he really was a poet. He had a volume of verse, *Dreamland and Other Poems*, with a publisher in Kingston, Ontario, where Sleight had studied at Queen's College, and where he had begun to make a name for himself as one of the poetic voices of modern Canada. The book was due to be off the printing presses soon.

Sleight used words the way she imagined a poet ought to—suddenly breaking loose from the humdrum of everyday conversation to unburden himself of a winging flight of fancy on the October afternoon, "with Nature's feathered children on the move across a sky suspended in time, whence summer has fled and winter is yet held back, when the throbbing colors of the sunset blaze forth in echo from the foliage, too beautiful to be denied, too perfect to last."

He came to call on Anna Lee, more than once. They went for a ride together through the October afternoon that he had rhapsodized over. Sleight had a buggy, such as the Canadians used, with grease in the axles so that it clipped along silently and gracefully.

He tried to kiss her in the buggy, outside of town, but she pulled back.

It was a reflex action at first, just what was expected of her as a chaste young woman. "Please . . . no!" and her hand up in front of her face. She was not at all sure that she meant 'no,' but it was the thing to say, at first. You could always say yes, later. But it was too late to say no once you had allowed it to be done.

"Come on, little lady, you know you want to," Sleight said. He took her by the wrist and pulled her hand away from her face, as he moved his own face closer to hers.

"No . . . no . . ." she murmured, and put up her other hand.

He grasped that wrist, too, but this time his grip was tighter, his motion more impatient.

And suddenly, Anna Lee felt panicked, and her voice rose sharply.

"No!"

She tried to twist away from Sleight, but he only held her wrists tighter, and forced her shoulders around so that her body was square to his, although she still ducked her head away.

She was certain, now, that she did not want him kissing her, or touching her in any other way. The panic rose in her, as she struggled to get away from him.

Sleight was not sweet-talking her now; he grunted from the exertion, as he tried to hold her arms apart and pull her body to him. She kept resisting, and kept ducking her head away. He had to let go of one wrist in order to grab her chin and pull her mouth up to his; and when he did that, she drew back her arm and slapped him hard, across the face.

Her hand stung, but she was not sure she had made any impression on him at all. She slapped him again, and this time he stopped struggling with her.

"I beg your pardon, dear child," he said stiffly, emphazing his cultured, urban accent for all it was worth. "I was overcome. I was not myself."

They rode back to Winnipeg in silence, and Sleight left her off at her mother's house.

Anna Lee thought about Henry Sleight that night, and over the next few days and nights. It was hard for her to understand what had happened. She knew that Sleight was supposed to be a model of refinement and sensitivity in this rough prairie town, but if she had not known it, she would have said that he seemed so . . . so insensitive.

Sleight did not call on her again for a week. She wondered if she had done the right thing in pushing him away. The memory, of the panic she had felt receded in her memory. And instead, she found herself thinking about being lonely, and having no handsome, sophisticated suitor in her life any more. There would have been nothing wrong in being kissed by a man who wanted to so ardently. Why had she pushed him away?

By the end of the week, she was looking at herself in the mirror and seeing nothing but ugly imperfections in her face. She did not think that he would ever come to see her again. She did not think that anyone would ever want to kiss her again.

But Sleight did come back into the store again, the next week. It was about eleven o'clock in the morning, a slow time for business. There were only a few customers there, and no one that Anna Lee was actually waiting on.

Her face lit up with a smile when Sleight walked in, clad in his familiar tweed knickers and high-laced boots, a deerstalker cap on his head, a hint of a swagger in his walk.

"Henry!" she called out gaily.

Sleight favored her with a small, tight smile, and tipped his cap. Then he set about closely examining a selection of hunting rifles, as Anna Lee shrank into herself, crestfallen.

She looked around the store, embarrassed, to see if the other customers had noticed the snub that Sleight had inflicted on her. They were all looking at Sleight, with what seemed to be open hostility.

She colored with embarrassment at first, and then realized that nobody was paying her the slightest attention. No, of course not, she thought. They can't all be angry at him for slighting me. But she could not imagine what it was that had upset them all so.

Henry Sleight was not ignoring only her. He was pointedly ignoring everyone in the store.

That was some consolation to her, but she felt even better when she realized that his studied refusal to take any notice of her at all was his way of flirting. He had, after all, come in knowing that she was there. And if she played her cards right, showed just enough interest without being too forward, he would eventually make his way over to her and begin talking to her.

She wished that she were more experienced, and knew the rules of this game better. Her palms were sweating, and her body felt tight with anxiety. But she did her best. She smiled when he caught her eye, and she tried not to look at him when he was not looking at her, so she would not seem to be the aggressor.

He moved on from the guns, and began fingering the flannel shirts, the red-and-black checked garments the *métis* wore, and which Henry Sleight would certainly not have been caught dead in.

All the time, there was still the other mood going on in the store, the one that had nothing to do with her: the waves of hostility directed towards Henry Sleight. Stony faces and muttered whispers.

Everyone seemed to feel it. The customers who made their purchases and left, cast sidelong glances over their shoulders at him as they paused at the door. New customers, just coming in, pulled up short when they recognized Sleight, and shot angry looks at him. And as Anna Lee continued to try to figure it all out, Sleight went on blithely ignoring it.

Finally, Sleight gave up examining the guns, the flannel shirts, the Bibles and bandanas and hunting knives. He looked up, as if noticing Anna Lee for the first time, and smiled at her.

She kept up her end of the pretense, and smiled back.

"Anna Lee, my dear, how are you?" he asked, ambling over toward her. "How have you been?"

"I've been fine," she said.

"I've been away from the settlement," he said with a vague wave of his hand. "Business . . . you know. A man must go where his calling takes him. I've thought of you . . ."

"That's very nice of you to say so," Anna Lee said with demure reserve.

"Oh, not at all," Sleight said. "In fact . . ."

"Sleight!" a voice behind him snapped.

Sleight turned around at the sound of his name, and Anna Lee looked up. She found herself confronted by a tall man, just under six feet, powerfully built with broad shoulders and big hands. His face was broad and handsome, and topped by wavy, dark brown hair that swept down his cheeks in luxuriant muttonchop sideburns.

His thick eyebrows were furrowed, his face intense, frowning, passionate, brooding. Only his dark eyes seemed incongruously calm, and touched with something like sadness. Anna Lee had never seen him before; she was quite certain of that, anyway.

She would never have forgotten him.

"You are Henry Sleight, are you not?" the stranger demanded.

"You have the advantage of me, sir," Sleight replied, "I am, in fact, Henry Sleight. And you . . . ?"

"One of your readers, Mr. Sleight."

Sleight cocked an eyebrow. "Of my verse?"

"Of the 'Epistles from the Frontier' that have begun appearing in the Toronto *Globe*."

"Ah, yes, of course." Sleight appeared to be enjoying the badinage, as near as Anna Lee could make out. But she was not, in any case, looking back and forth between the two men to gauge their expressions.

She was only looking at the newcomer. For her, Henry Sleight might as well have ceased to exist.

But for the stranger, it seemed, she might as well not have existed. If he had even noticed she was there, he had not shown it.

She leaned forward over the counter a little, not quite into the line of fire between them, but at least—she hoped—into his peripheral vision.

"Ah, yes, the 'Epistles from the Frontier,' " Sleight said, "I should have realized. Not nearly as aesthetically demanding—much more in the popular style, accessible to provincial readers."

"What were the 'Epistles from the Frontier?' " Anna Lee asked.

The stranger now turned and looked at her, and her heart trembled. But he was still caught up in his outrage, and he pounded the counter with the rolled-up newspaper he held in his hand.

"What? You haven't heard about Mr. Sleight's famous evaluation of the Red River settlement and its people, from the point of view of a sophisticate from the great Canadian centers of culture?"

He began to read: " 'Upon my arrival I put up at the Winnipeg Hotel, but after a few days I went over and stayed at Dr. Schultz's. The change was comfortable, I assure you, from the racket of a motley crowd of half-breeds, playing billiards and drinking, to the quiet and solid comfort of a home. I was invited to a dinner party at Beggs, with the Governor's brother-in-law, a wealthy merchant here named Mrs. Graham, and other Nor-Westers. Altogether, I received hospitalities to my heart's content, and left the place thoroughly pleased with most that I met.

" *'There are jealousies and heartburnings, however. Many wealthy people are married to half-breed women who, having no coat of arms but a totem pole to look back to, make up for the deficiency by biting at the backs of their white sisters. The white sisters fall back on their whiteness, whilst the husbands meet each other with desperate courtesies and hospitalities, with a view of filthy lucre in the background.'* "

Sleight stood uncomfortably, listening to his own words. He straightened up stiffly when the other had finished, and sniffed.

Anna Lee was embarrassed to hear her mother's name mentioned in such a context, but mostly, she was shocked at the social and racial snobbery Sleight had expressed.

"How could you say such things, Henry?" she asked.

"Hyperbole . . . poetic license," Sleight said. "But certainly it can come as no surprise to you, my dear, that the provinces are . . . well, shall we say . . . provincial?"

"Is Mr. Sleight a friend of yours, miss?" the stranger asked.

"Is he . . . well, yes, but not . . . I certainly don't approve of this!"

"I was very kind to your mother in it, Anna Lee."

"Your mother?"

"Yes," Anna Lee said. "My mother is Mrs. Graham.

But that doesn't make any difference in how I feel, and I'm sure it wouldn't make any difference to my mother, either."

Sleight turned to face his accuser, still looking supercilious. "Is there anything you wanted to add on this subject, sir? Because if not, I'll . . ."

"I'd like to jam this newspaper down your throat, you swine!"

"I'm willing to let you try it, if you think you could."

"Oh, please don't!" Anna Lee said.

The stranger glared at her, and she grew flustered. She certainly did not want him to think she was defending Sleight. He probably already thought that, because of the way her mother had been treated in the article. "I mean . . . in here . . . my mother's store. . . ."

"Dr. John Schultz's store!" the stranger said.

"Well, yes . . . but I'll be held responsible for it, if anything gets broken . . ."

From the way he was looking at her, Anna Lee was afraid that he still did not approve of her. And from the way she was looking at him . . . well, she just could not stop looking at him. That was all there was to that.

He was so somber, so serious, from his dark clothes to his frowning mouth to his sad eyes. Was it just because he was angry? Did he ever smile?

He was seething now, trying to bring his temper back under control, trying to settle down.

"All right," he said, very slowly, making each word a separate sentence. "No fight. No violence. Not in here, anyway."

Sleight brushed a speck of lint off the sleeve of his tweed suit, and straightened his shoulders again. He gave the clear impression that he assumed he had won, and now was waiting for his adversary to leave the field.

Sleight was waiting, now, for the moment he had been

maneuvering for all along—the chance to talk to Anna Lee alone, after he had gotten her on tenterhooks. But that moment had come and gone, without his having taken advantage of it. Now she only wanted him out of there.

The door opened again, and a woman of about sixty walked in. Anna Lee knew her well. Her name was Suzanne Richards. She was the wife of the local postmaster, a spunky, active little old lady who got around the territory on horseback, helped her husband out with the mails, knew and was known by everyone in the territory. She had on a widebrimmed hat and the leather skirt she wore for riding, and she carried a horsewhip under her arm.

"I declare, it's a beautiful, invigorating day out, Anna Lee," she said. "I've just come down from St. Boniface way, and loved every minute of it. You should get out in the open air more, a healthy young girl like yourself. Do some riding. Get out and . . ."

She stopped short, and when she spoke again, the open friendliness had drained out of her voice, and been replaced by cold anger. "Oh, Mr. Sleight, is it?"

Sleight gave a polite bow. "Madam," he said.

"Don't madam me! Bowing to my face and writing garbage like that about the Red River women behind our backs—is that what English gentlemen do? Well, here's how we treat the sort of gentleman out on the frontier!"

Suddenly, the old lady advanced on Sleight, unlimbering her horsewhip from where she had it tucked under arm.

"Madam, I . . ." Sleight began, but she was on top of him, flailing away at him with the horsewhip, as he put up his hands to try and ward off the blows.

The stranger stepped nimbly out of the way, and Mrs. Richards kept right on horsewhipping the tweedy Englishman, until he backed rapidly toward the door.

"And you'd better send someone else after your mail,

because if I ever see you near the Post Office again, you'll be getting more of this!''

Sleight left the door open behind him as he fled.

The other man watched him go. He walked over to the empty doorframe and looked down the street at Sleight's retreating form.

''And Mr. Sleight, your verse is a pallid, sentimental imitation of Dryden, with faltering rhythms and weak prosody,'' he said.

He turned to Mrs. Richards, and saluted her with a gesture that brought the tips of his fingers up to his forehead. Then he threw back his head, and began to laugh.

The laughter rumbled up from inside of him. It was not the sound of a man who laughed often, but it was hearty, and it rolled out of him freely. He caught Anna Lee's eye for a moment as he was laughing, and she smiled with pure joy to be sharing the moment with him. Then he put on his hat, and walked out of the store, still laughing.

Suzanne Richards' anger was under control now. She breathed deeply, and grinned at Anna Lee. ''Well, I don't do that every day,'' she said, looking coyly pleased with herself.

''Who was that, Mrs. Richards?'' Anna Lee asked.

''Why, Henry Sleight. You know that as well as I do.''

''No, the other man.''

''Oh, that was Louis Riel—the son of Louis Riel who led the fur traders for their rights against the Hudson's Bay Company. He's just back from Canada. He's been to university in Montreal, studying for the priesthood. He's a brilliant one, they say. Moody, but brilliant. He was deep even as a lad, well I remember.''

''He's a priest?'' Anna Lee tried not to look too obviously crestfallen.

''No, he stopped short of that. He dropped out of the seminary. It wasn't his calling, I guess. There's some as are called to it, and some as are not. He's got a calling of some sort, I'm sure of that. He's a deep one, and no mistake. Deep and intense, always serious. He's a *métis*. Doesn't look like it, with that pale skin of his, but he is. Well, as I said, his father was Louis Riel, senior, so of course he's a *métis*. Well, I'd best be getting along. Put these things on my bill, there's a good girl, and I'll try to behave myself the next time I come in here. Though if that Henry Sleight is around again, I'm not promising anything. Goodbye, dear."

Louis Riel. And he was not a priest. And he lived in Red River . . . he had come back home. And he could laugh, after all.

She pictured him laughing that night, as she lay in bed. And she pictured him not laughing, too. She pictured him very close to her, and looking into her eyes. She could see his eyes vividly: those sad, calm eyes, deep in that intense face. It was the last image on her mind when she fell asleep, and it was the image in her dreams.

8

THAT evening, Henry Sleight licked his wounds at the home of Dr. John Schultz.

"I never thought they'd take on so," he complained. "Dammit, I never even thought they'd see the letters. Why should anyone be getting the Toronto newspapers out here in Red River, anyway?"

"Who would even have thought that they could read?" Schultz observed dryly.

Sleight did not appear to appreciate the witticism. His brow was still furrowed, and he did not look comfortable. "I don't know about that," he said. "But even if they read it, I don't see why they should have to carry on so about it. I mean, it was all in fun. What's the matter—can't they take a joke?"

"They're a bunch of ignorant louts," Schultz told him. "Here, your glass is empty. Have another."

The neck of the glass bottle clicked against the rim of the glass tumbler in Sleight's hand, and good Scotch whiskey poured from the one to the other. The aroma filled Sleight's nostrils, and reminded him of the cultural difference between Dr. John Schultz's house and the rest of the Red River settlement.

Schultz tilted the bottle back upright, and set it on the table.

Sleight turned his glass on an angle, and watched as the liquid retained its parallel level to the table, to the floor, to the hard earth of the Red River settlement below that. He shook the glass, and the whiskey became little waves that eventually took to swirling around in circles. Then he took a drink, and let the taste roll around in his mouth the same way.

"It doesn't mean a thing," Schultz told him. "You don't have to pay any attention to what those savages say. They don't have feelings."

"That's easy enough for you to say," Sleight told him. "You're not the one who was horsewhipped."

Schultz shrugged. "I have had worse than that happen to me. Don't let it throw you."

Sleight looked at Schultz dubiously, as if trying to imagine what could have happened to him at the hands of an outraged populace that was worse than horsewhipping. Schultz saw the doubt in his eyes.

"You listen to me, young fellow," he admonished him. "You've got a reputation now that can do you some good. People will know you're a gent to be reckoned with. If you run around trying to apologize to every half-breed in every tent on the prairie, no one will believe you anyway. They still won't trust you, and they won't respect you either. We can't have it. It's respect that we've got to instill into the hearts of these savages—respect and fear. Remember, there's a wide-open country out here and a lot of money to be made by those of us who get to it first—if we do it right."

"I suppose so . . ."

"And if you want to get laid, don't worry about that. There are plenty of half-breed whores around who'll do the job just as well for you."

There was a dance that Saturday night at the Dutchman's hotel, that same hotel which Henry Sleight had disparaged in his letter to the Toronto *Globe*. It was a special celebration, but along the frontier they usually had very little trouble thinking up a special celebration that called for a dance. It was the favorite form of recreation. Winnipeg had a regular band by then, to play for their dances—two fiddles, a guitar, and a washboard, and Leo Laprade, an old, white-bearded former fur trader who called out the dance steps in a cracked but sprightly voice, and stomped out the rhythm on the wooden peg that took the place of the leg he had left in a beaver trap fifteen years before.

The dance was a celebration of the end of pemmican making for the year. The night was clear and cold, and Anna Lee looked over her shoulder at the new moon, and wondered if Louis Riel would be there, and hoped that Henry Sleight would not.

She was lucky on both counts. The Dutchman had threatened to break Sleight's head if he ever set foot in the hotel again, so that was no surprise. But her heart leapt when she saw Riel.

He was shy. Still fresh out of the seminary, he appeared to be ill-at-ease with the idea of dancing, and he hovered back in a corner. But he was there.

The dancing got under way, with the band alternating white American dance music, reels and square dances, with the slow, hypnotic Indian dances. The young people danced to the former. The older *métis* women danced every dance, but they danced alone, and always the same slow, stately figures of their own dances, whatever tune the musicians were playing.

Riel never got near the dance floor. But he stayed, all through the evening—at least he was not getting bored and wandering off into the night. She felt that if he had tried to leave, before she had her chance with him, she would have run out and tackled him on the spot.

She kept her eye on him, or, when she was too shy, she had her friend Marie-Catherine keep her eye on him, and report back to her. When she watched herself, she knew that he knew. And occasionally, she would see him glancing back in her direction.

Finally, she knew it was time. The fiddlers raised their bows, and began to play the introductory notes to "Sweet Rosalie."

"Now!" Anna Lee nudged Marie-Catherine. "Ask him to dance."

"You ask him," Marie-Catherine said, but Anna Lee silenced her with that air of authority that only the truly obsessed can muster.

"You ask him."

And that was that. Everything happened quickly then, so quickly there was no time to think about it. Marie-Catherine's hand was on Louis Riel's wrist, and she was dragging him out to the dance floor. Anna Lee had a partner, and she lined up in the same circle, across from Riel.

His eyes sought hers now, bewildered. He knew that she was responsible for whatever was going on. But what was going on?

Laprade began, in his scratchy voice, singing out the dance step instructions to "Sweet Rosalie." The dancers joined hands, swayed in a circle to the left, then to the right. They dropped hands, clapped in rhythm, and sang along with Laprade:

La Belle Rosalie va au centre . . .

and the leader of the dance, the man at the head of the circle, pushed the woman to his right—"Sweet Rosalie"—into the middle. Then, as the rest of the dancers continued clapping, they sang along with Leo Laprade:

Embrassez que vous voudrez
Car j'aurai la moitee

and "Sweet Rosalie" went up to the man of her choice and kissed him *a la mode du pays*, as they called it, after the custom of the country. And the custom of the country was a firm kiss right on the lips.

Then the girl went back and stood on the left of the leader, and the dance began again, with a new girl on the leader's right, a new "Sweet Rosalie."

As soon as the first round of the dance reached its climax, Riel understood what was going on. His face turned beet red, and he looked around to either side, as if hoping to find an escape. When he looked across at Anna Lee, her eyes were sparkling with laughter. She looked straight back at him, enjoying his embarrassment, biding her time and waiting her turn.

She would be the third "Sweet Rosalie."

The song went through another round, the second "Sweet Rosalie" placed her kiss on her chosen one's lips. Then the song started again, and then it was Anna Lee's turn in the center of the circle.

Embrassez que vous voulez . . .

She spun around, made a couple of feints in one direction, then another, and finally skipped over to Louis Riel. She stood on tiptoe, put both hands up to his cheeks to pull his face down to hers, and kissed him—very much *a la mode du pays*.

Things started happening to her body that she had never experienced before. Electricity coursed through her, from her lips to her toes, and her brain whirled.

She only held the kiss for an instant, but she was having trouble breathing when she pulled away, and she felt dizzy. For a moment, she could not even find her way back across the circle to the left side of the leader.

The whole social hall had erupted with cheers, whistles, and hoots. Dazed as she was by the kiss, it took Anna Lee a few seconds to realize what was going on, but then she did. Those last few steps back out of the center seemed endless, and the oil lamps around the periphery of the hall suddenly seemed to have coalesced into one blinding halo of light right above her head.

She finally made it back, and turned around to stand in her place, but with her head bowed and her eyes lowered, half-closed.

When she finally got up the courage to raise her head, the hooting and whistling was still going on. She saw Louis across from her, blushing and gesturing in an ineffectual way to try and deflect the cheering. Looking around at some of the other faces in the room, and seeing the way attention was being showered on him, she began to realize two things. First, what a popular person Louis Riel was in his community. And second, that everyone knew what she had suspected—that it was the young ex-seminarian's first kiss.

She would have liked to seize the opportunity to slip away with him late in the evening. The stars were still ablaze in the sky, the new moon high over Red River like a sliver of hope. But there would be no slipping away that night. A hundred pairs of eyes would have followed them all the way.

* * *

She played the scene over and over again her mind that night. Had she played her cards wrong? Perhaps she had embarrassed him too much. If only she had been able to talk to him alone afterwards. Perhaps he would never see her again, Perhaps . . .

But on the other hand, she was sure of one thing, as sure as her intuition could make her.

He had felt that one kiss as powerfully as she had.

The next day, he came to call. Once again, he wore a dark suit, and looked for all the world like a young priest. But the look in his face was anything but priestly. Even his sad, still eyes glowed with a passion that was not something he had learned at the seminary.

She took the afternoon off from the store, and they went riding together. After a while, some distance out of town, they tethered their horses to a tree and walked, close together but not touching.

"Was Montreal exciting?" Anna Lee asked him.

"The university was."

"Why did you decide to come back?"

"I was needed."

"By your family?"

"By my family, yes. My father died while I was away."

"I'm sorry."

"It's all right—it was a few years ago. My mother got along for a while, running the sawmill that Papa owned. But I know I can help her out, being home. But there was more, too . . . you know that my father was a great and respected leader of the *métis* people."

"Yes, I know that."

"These are bad times in Red River. There's talk of the Hudson's Bay Company selling the whole area to Canada. And if that happens, there's no safeguard for anyone's title to his land. Not with men like your friends Dr. John

Schultz and Henry Sleight around to take what they can get, and to blazes with who was there already."

"They're not my friends," Anna Lee said.

"John Schultz is your mother's partner," Riel said fiercely, twitching with an emotion so intense that it frightened her.

"I don't believe everything my mother believes," she said. "Just because Dr. Schultz is her partner, doesn't mean that I go along with what she believes. I don't even know anything about it. So if you want me to know what to believe, you can tell me."

He did not answer. He seemed to be a little mollified but still disturbed over something. He hunched his shoulders up, drew his head down between them like a turtle, and kept on walking.

"And you've been keeping company with Henry Sleight," he said.

"That's not true! Who's been telling you that?" She said hotly. *He's been asking about me*, she thought delightedly.

"I heard it was true," Riel said doggedly.

"I . . . I did let him call on me once or twice, but that's all. I don't care anything about Henry Sleight."

He did not answer once again, but this time he seemed to be more mollified. He came out of his shell, just a little bit. He straightened up, and walked with a lighter step.

"Why did you leave the seminary?" Anna Lee asked him.

"It wasn't for me to do. You can't study for the priesthood without taking it seriously."

"Did you take it very seriously, then?"

He gave a short laugh. "That's what they tell me. The other seminarians used to say I was studying to be St. Peter."

He laughed again, but it was forced, the sort of laugh

one gives at something one has been told is funny, and ought to be laughed at. Joking did not come easily to him. "And why not?" he said fiercely. "The priesthood is a great calling, and it should be taken seriously. And so is the calling I came back to here—the cause of my people."

"They really need you here," Anna Lee said. She did not entirely understand what she was talking about, but she felt absolutely sure that they must need him here—this strange, brooding, fearsome, exciting man. She knew that she needed him here.

"These are hard times," he said.

"I'm glad you came back here," she said. She wanted to slip her arm through his, but she was afraid to be so forward. She could only wait, and be prepared to do whatever he wanted.

"The world is full of temptation," he said, in a voice so choked with emotional turmoil that he could hardly get the words out.

"Oh, but if you're not going to be a priest, it's not the same, is it?" she said.

She turned to face him at the same instant that he turned, and two pairs of arms opened up and curled back around bodies that were already pressed together, as close as they could be, until the embrace pulled them even closer.

He was covering her face with kisses, all over. She felt bathed in them, transported by them, baptised in them. But she wanted to kiss him, too, and she stopped his lips with her own, and kept them from drifting away again, as she kissed him over and over.

She lost all sense of time. But somehow, at some point, they went from standing and holding each other to lying down together on the ground, the weight of his body on top of hers bringing them closer yet.

She was doing things, actually doing them, that she had scarcely even done in fantasy before—that perhaps had not even occurred to her, until she had first set eyes on Louis Riel.

Her clothes fell away, and her naked body was pressed against his dark suit. This was truly a sensation she had never imagined, not even in her dreams, and it made her breathless.

Louis could not get enough of her, His hands, his mouth covered her hungrily. His body heaved and pressed and wriggled to touch her more. He was muttering under his breath, and with his breath, guttural and heavy noises. He sounded almost angry, and Anna Lee was as awed as she was excited by him.

He fumbled with his trousers, and a moment later his penis, hard and smooth, was pressing against her thigh. Almost as soon as it touched her, she felt something wet, hot, and sticky spatter her inner thigh. She did not know what it was; it felt strange, but it did not bother her. She accepted it as part of this wonderful new experience, all of which was strange to her.

But it was tremendously upsetting to Louis. He uttered an angry oath, and rolled off her.

She was confused. Feeling suddenly very naked, she sat up, holding her arms across her chest.

"What is it, Louis?" she asked.

"It's wrong . . . it's wrong . . ." he said.

"It's not wrong," she said, reaching for his hand. "I wanted you to."

"No, not that," he said. "It's . . ."

"Come here. Come back, Louis," she said, pulling gently on his hand. "Come and lie with me . . . I need you, Louis, I really do."

"I can't," he said, close to tears now.

But she pulled on his hand again, and he drew closer to her. He lay down beside her and touched her again, tentatively at first.

Without knowing why, Anna Lee knew that somehow she was older and wiser and more experienced than her lover, and that it was up to her to be patient with him, to teach him what she herself did not know, or was just learning. She slid her fingers through the curly hair at the back of his neck, and pulled his head down to the softness of her beast. She kissed his forehead, and the top of his head, and murmured to him—not words, just a gentle flow of loving encouragement, in a soft, breathy tone.

Gradually, he began moving on her again. His breath got heavier again, and she could feel his excitement beginning to infect her once more.

He lay on top of her again, and this time, as her thighs opened, she could feel his penis, hard once more, butting up at the area between them. She reached down, and took it with her hand, and guided it to the spot that called for it with such intensity of feeling that it could not be denied.

She screamed for just an instant at a pain that she had not expected, the feeling of something tearing inside her. And in that instant, panic seized her and she was afraid that she had done it terribly wrong.

But the panic was over as quickly as it had come, and she knew that she had gotten it right.

They stayed there all afternoon, until it was growing dark. Then they found a stream and washed up, and Louis brought her home.

"Why don't you come in and visit for a little while here?" Anna Lee asked him.

"No, I can't," he said hastily. "I'd be . . . well, I'll see you again soon. Tomorrow, maybe."

"Tomorrow," she said. She kissed him *à la mode du pays*, and went in the house.

9

FOR some reason, it did not occur to Anna Lee until she was actually inside the door, with her mother and brother looking at her, that she was supposed to feel furtive and embarrassed.

Then it hit her like a thunderclap. Her fingers went weak, and the door slipped out of her hand, slamming shut behind her like a jail cell. She realized all of a sudden why Louis had not wanted to come in, and she wished she were with him—or even not with him: *anywhere*, so long as she was out of this house and away from these people.

"How was your afternoon with Mr. Riel, dear?" Charlotte asked. "Did you have a pleasant time?"

"Y . . . yes, quite pleasant, Mama," Anna Lee managed to say, and hearing the sound of her own voice somehow reconnected some inner circuitry of her nervous system, and steadied her. She calmed down the quaver that she had started out with, and continued smoothly. "We took a ride together, and talked about Mr. Riel's experiences.

He is a very interesting man, you know. He went to the university in Montreal, and he is learned on a great variety of subjects."

"Yes, so I've heard. And his father helped your father and the other fur traders, years back."

"I know."

"Of course, those were wilder, ruder times. We were truly living on the frontier, and frontier methods were sometimes necessary to get justice. But that's all different now. Red River is practically Canada."

"Yes, Mama."

"Tell me, Anna Lee, how is Mr. Sleight?"

"Oh, I haven't seen him recently. Not since . . ."

"Yes, yes," Charlotte said impatiently. She had heard about the horsewhipping already, had voiced her disapproval of Mrs. Richards' action strongly, and had pronounced the matter closed, as far as she was concerned.

Anna Lee felt as if she were two people, and she was exhilarated by the feeling. One of them was sitting in this room with her mother, talking as coolly and calmly as she might have on any other day. The other—the one that was the real Anna Lee—was some distance back, watching it all. The real Anna Lee marveled at this girl's ability to carry off such a deception with no practice, no forewarning, and to do so as easily as if she had been doing it all her life.

Meanwhile, all the time that this was going on, the real Anna Lee was free to wander out of the house in her mind, back to the hillside where she could taste again the kisses of her lover, and feel him suddenly inside her body, that body which had been hers alone and was now part of him, and he part of it.

While she talked to her mother, James was looking at her darkly, through eyes narrowed into slits. He did not say anything, and Anna Lee did not know what he was thinking, but she knew that it was no good, as far as she was concerned. She avoided looking at him, and concentrated instead on talking to her mother.

He caught her alone, later. He came to her room, after she had put on her nightgown and gone to bed.

"What are you doing in here?" she hissed at him in a whisper. "Get out my bedroom. I've already gone to bed."

"What difference should that make to you?" he whispered back, bitterly. "I haven't seen that you've been so particular lately."

"What in heaven's name are you talking about?" Anna Lee demanded.

"You know."

"I don't know."

"I was there this afternoon. I saw you tethering your horses, and I followed you."

"You little sneak . . .!"

"You've got no right to say anything to me. You filthy, disgusting . . ."

"You don't know what you're talking about. You can't know. You're just a child. You've never been in love."

"Don't give me any of that. It's just disgusting, that's all."

"Shut up!"

"And how could you . . . with a half-breed? How could you let one of them put his filthy, greasy, disgusting hands on you?"

"Stop it, James!"

"I won't stop it! A filthy, greasy half-breed. Don't you know who you are? Don't you know who our family is? Even if you don't care anything about yourself, you should have that much consideration for the rest of us."

"Don't you know who you are?" Anna Lee blazed

out, now completely overcome with anger. "Everybody knows—"

She caught herself, and stopped.

And a dead calm suddenly came over the room.

"Everybdoy knows what?"

Anna Lee stayed silent, and she realized that she was fighting tears. She was about to say something out loud that she had never even permitted herself to formulate in her mind before. A rumor that she had heard whispered obliquely, never directly.

"Everybody knows what?" James asked again, and Anna Lee began to cry.

"You aren't going to tell Mama, are you?" she asked.

James continued to stare at her. He did not speak again, but she knew that he was still asking her the same question: *Everybody knows what?*

"Please . . ." she said. "Please don't tell Mama."

James turned and stalked out of the room without saying another word.

10

LOUIS Riel began calling on Anna Lee regularly. Henry Sleight, to Charlotte's extreme disappointment, was no longer coming to call on her. Riel was formally courting her.

He came to call on her at home. Then, he asked if he could be her escort at the next dance. Anna Lee Graham and Louis Riel were the new couple in Winnipeg, the two whom everyone gossiped about. "How is Louis?" became the first question that anyone put to Anna Lee; and "how is Anna Lee?" was high up on the list of questions that Louis heard when he came into town, especially from the women.

Anna Lee was thrilled to be in the position she now found herself in. And even her mother had to go along with this new arrangement, however grudgingly she did so in private.

Louis Riel was not the sort of man that Charlotte had wanted for her only daughter.

But Charlotte knew that she did not quite have the social

standing to insist that her daughter stop seeing Louis Riel. She wished that Anna Lee had waited a little longer to grow up. Charlotte was gaining in social standing, the sort of social standing that money and power can bring in a new society. Her business partnership with Dr. John Schultz was helping to insure that. But she was still not on a social level with the new white families from Canada, the officers and their wives from Fort Garry, and the high-level officials of the Hudson's Bay Company who had brought their families out and settled in the area where their profits came from, becoming the governing and law enforcing class of the territory.

Charlotte could not be exclusive. She had to deal with the *métis* all the time. She was, after all, in trade, and the *métis* families were still the overwhelming majority in the community—not that there were really any reasonable alternatives to Charlotte Graham's general store, if they wanted to get the goods they needed to survive the winters, to do their planting, to get cooking utensils or cloth to make clothes or brooms to sweep out their houses.

But she had to maintain some semblance of community relations. And the Reils were among the most respected families in the *métis* community. It would create real problems for her, if she were to insist that her daughter stop seeing Louis.

There was only one other drawback to Anna Lee's happiness. Now that their courtship was public, there was no more opportunity for Louis and her to get away by themselves, the way they had done the first wonderful, idyllic afternoon.

Anna Lee's body ached for him. She had spent one exquisite, perfect afternoon locked in his embrace, and she craved more with every nerve ending that tingled under her skin, every vein and artery that sent blood pumping hot and wild into her heart, and back out again to every extremity.

Every time they were together she felt it, an ache that drew her to him like a magnet, demanding that she touch him to be satisfied.

And she could not do it. Not until they were married—unless, somehow, the public eye could slip off them again and they could find away to steal away and be alone together.

But that did not seem likely, not the way things were. Louis was so involved with meetings, councils, people who needed him to solve one problem or another, that his time with Anna Lee was limited.

Then, too, Louis still had his strict seminarian's conscience. And after that one passionate outburst, it seemed to be in the ascendant over his libido. He respected her virtue too much, he told her, to compromise her again while they were not officially united in the sight of God.

Where Louis was concerned, Anna Lee had no virtue, only her aching, overwhelming need. But she could not convince him of that—in fact, she did not even dare to talk to him about it very much. He was unyielding in his principles, and he was just as unyielding in the moral demands that he held them both to.

Well, if he was going to be a pillar of virtue, she could be too, she supposed. After all, she knew that it was the good and proper way, especially for a young lady. She had never questioned those values, before she had met Louis.

But she wanted him. That was the new factor in her view of life. And she knew that, whatever he might say, he wanted her too.

Dr. John Schultz was not at all happy with the idea of his partner's daughter becoming romantically involved with a *métis*, and he did not hold back from making his disapproval clear.

"I can't help it, Dr. Schultz," Charlotte told him. "I can't antagonize the *métis* community the way I would if I were to forbid Anna Lee to see Louis Riel. We have to live with the *métis*, whether we like it or not. They're the majority here."

"We don't have to do anything whether we like it or not, Mrs. Graham," Schultz replied. "Never. Do you understand me?"

"Yes, but . . ."

"There are no *buts*, Mrs. Graham. Not if we expect to be strong, and face our destiny squarely. It's up to us to decide what we like, and then it's up to us to make it happen. We're white, and we're Canadian. We represent the future of this territory. There's going to be progress here—a real civilization! A new influx of settlers from Canada, and you know what I mean there, Mrs. Graham. I mean white settlers, with a culture instead of tribal customs, with morals and values and capital for investment. There will be the chance for real land development! Mrs. Graham, I had damn well thought that you, of all people in this settlement, were a woman of vision."

"My vision is just fine, Dr. Schultz," Charlotte replied, stung and chastised. "And so is my understanding of what is in Red River, and what can be. Don't worry about that."

"It isn't if you can see a half-breed son-in-law in your own family," Schultz sneered. "Think about that, Mrs. Graham."

"Oh, I'm not at all sure it will go that far," Charlotte said. She had felt intimidated, but now she gained confidence again. She was back on a woman's familiar ground now, a mother's ground, talking about matters that she understood much better than did the doctor. "Time and circumstance could tear that union apart very easily—

especially if even half of what you're talking about comes to pass."

"It'll come to pass," growled the doctor.

"Then let's just wait and see what happens between my daughter and her hot-headed, principled young man. It may not be at all what you think."

"I hope you're right."

"Now who's relying on hope? Don't worry—you can do a great deal more than hope, partner. You can count on it. Which reminds me—are we still buying the local newspaper?"

"The *Nor'Wester*? Yes, we take possession in three weeks. Henry Sleight will be the new editor, and we can count on the slant of the paper to be . . . shall we say, just what it ought to be?"

"Oh, don't make Henry Sleight the editor of the paper," Charlotte said so casually that it was impossible to tell whether it was an idea, that had just occurred to her, or part of a long-held plan.

"Why not?"

"Dr. Schultz, we are buying up and taking over the only newspaper in the territory—a newspaper that is presently owned and edited by a *métis*, and expresses the *métis* point of view. When we take over its management, and with the new editorial policy that we'll be instituting, the new editor of the Nor'Wester will be the most hated man in the Red River settlement."

"Next to me."

"Next to you. And only for the time being, until we change the character of the Red River settlement to our liking. But for the time being, the editor of the *Nor'Wester* will be at least the second most hated man in the Red River settlement, and I don't want that to be Henry. Trust me."

Schultz lit a cigar, and considered the glowing end of it

thoughtfully. "Mmm," he said. "You could be right. Very well, then, I've got another man coming out here in a couple of weeks who's got some journalistic experience. Name's Philip Seldon. I can make him the most hated man in the Red River settlement, if you think that would suit you better."

"That suits me fine."

"All right, then, Philip Seldon is the editor of the *Nor'Wester*, and Henry Sleight can go back to being kind to puppy dogs and little old ladies, not that he's had much success in that regard around these parts, from what I hear."

"He's been more politic since then. But it's not the little *old* ladies I'm worried about, if you get my point, Dr. Schultz."

"Yes, quite. You make yourself most clear. Well, shall we drink to it?"

He poured two small glasses of sherry, handed one of them to Charlotte, and lifted his own glass toward hers in a toast.

"Here's to the new *Nor'Wester*, and to Philip Seldon, the most hated man in the whole Northwest, present company excepted, of course."

Charlotte raised her glass. "And to Henry Sleight, whatever the future may hold in store for him."

11

EVERYBODY knew that Dr. John Schultz had bought the *Nor'Wester*, and that the new version of the paper was going to be very different. Everybody in the Red River settlement was waiting for the first issue with the same anticipation that one feels for a major but unpleasant social event—a party given by a judge who has just sentenced six people to hang, or a wake for a rich old relative who has almost certainly disinherited everybody, or a wedding between the children of two families who have hated each other for generations.

Anna Lee felt the tension with particular sharpness. She had come to understand more and more, through her relationship with Louis, the fears of the *métis* community. The coming annexation of the territory by Canada, if and when it happened, could prove to be nothing more than an excuse for a ruthless land grab. There was no reason to count on a new Candian government's granting any recognition to the land titles that had been granted to local residents by the Hudson's Bay Company, which after all was not even a sovereign government. The *métis* farmers might very easily lose everything that they had built up and worked for.

Even the Scottish farmers were worried about what annexation might bring. No one had consulted them, either. So the two communities, which were often quite removed from communication with each other, were brought together in anxiety and distrust.

Why? Riel would ask Anna Lee over and over again, with a passionate anger that she experienced as keenly as if it had been directed against her.

"Why has Dr. John Schultz decided to open a real estate office in Winnipeg?"

"I don't know . . ."

"Since when do we need one? And who does he think will do business with him? The *métis?*"

"No . . ."

"The farmers?"

"No . . ."

"Can you think of anyone who owns land in Red River now, who does not hate and distrust him?"

"I suppose not . . ."

"You know that there isn't anyone. So why a real estate office. What is he up to? You tell me. Come on, Anna Lee—tell me. What do you think?"

"I don't know . . ."

"You're not that stupid, are you? You must have some opinion. What is your mother's friend Dr. John Schultz up to? What are the two of them up to?"

Anna Lee never had an answer to these harangues. It can't be that bad, it just can't be, she wanted to say. He wouldn't . . . nobody could . . . but she knew that she could never say anything like that to Louis. He would only become enraged at her, and accuse her of being on Dr. John Schultz's side.

After all, one thing was true, and she could not deny it: her mother was Schultz's partner.

So all she could do, when he got in those moods, was to cry. All she could do was to say: "Please, Louis . . . please don't. I don't understand any of what you're saying . . . maybe I am stupid, I can't help it . . . all I know is that I love you and it hurts me to see you angry. Please don't be angry."

It was all she could say, and it would always have the same effect on him. He would just accuse her all over again of being stupid. She knew that when he thought she was stupid, that made him angry too. But it was better than having him think that she was standing up for his enemies.

The first issue of the new *Nor'Wester* carried a front page editorial calling for the annexation of the Red River settlement by Canada. It was signed with editor Philip Seldon's name, but everyone who read it could see the fine sensibility of Dr. John Schultz at work, guiding Seldon's hand across the paper, fitting the leaded type into the rack, imprinting the words onto every issue of the *Nor'Wester* that came off the presses and made its way into the hands of Red River's residents.

Anna Lee read one paragraph over and over. She wished that she had never seen it, but she knew that there was no escaping it, or its implications to her own life, and to Louis Riel's feelings toward her:

"The wise and prudent will be prepared," the editorial ran, "to receive and to benefit from the coming influx of settlers; whilst the indolent, the careless, like the native tribes of the country, will fall back before the march of superior intelligence. Fall back they must—or be kept as cart drivers to bring in the vehicles of the new immigrants."

The indolent . . . the careless . . . native tribes . . . march of superior intelligence . . . it was all too hateful to be believed.

But if it was hateful to her, she could not even bear to think what it would be like to Louis. She spent long, solitary, sleepless nights imagining Louis's response to such a creed of hatred and bigotry.

She was all alone in her misery. There was no one to understand, no one to confide in or discuss it with. She did not, would not, talk to her mother about it, and her mother did not bring it up either.

James, on the other hand, would have been glad to talk about it, but Anna Lee would not have anything to do with him and his attitudes. He was belligerently gleeful as he sat at the dinner table and read aloud from the pages of the *Nor'Wester*. He had suddenly developed a passion for reading the local newspaper, which had never been remotely within his sphere of interest before.

"All my friends think it's about time we had someone telling the truth about the way things are around here," he said, smirking at Anna Lee. "Hurrah for the new *Nor'Wester!*"

"You don't have any friends, you little snake," Anna Lee told him.

"I do, too!"

"Oh? Who'd have anything to do with the likes of you? Nobody I know."

"The only people you know are half-breed scum, filthy, immoral mongrel dogs, the lot of 'em. I've got all the friends I need, and I'll have more, you can count on it, when some decent people start moving into Red River."

"Hah!"

"Sure, go on and laugh. Let's see you laugh when it

starts happening. Yes, and your precious Louis will be driving carts for them, too. And so will you."

"Shut up!"

"Cart driver, cart driver, cart driver!"

"Mother, make him stop!"

"James, stop teasing your sister."

"*Cart driver!*" James mouthed at her, as Charlotte was looking the other way.

"Mother, he's still doing it!"

"James, I meant it."

"Tell him it's not true, Mama, what he's saying. It's not true! It's not!"

"Anna Lee, you know you have to stop arguing with James, if you want him to stop teasing you," Charlotte said. "Fair is fair."

"Mother . . ."

But it was no use. She was never going to take a side, and Anna Lee knew it. She would never admit that there were real issues involved in the arguments between her two children.

Anna Lee was not going to pursue it, in any case. She was too afraid of which side her mother would take, if Anna Lee finally forced her into taking a side between them.

So quietly, all by herself, she waited, and prepared herself for the rage that Louis would direct at her, when he saw her next.

She prepared herself for days. And only gradually did the other, and far more horrible, possibility begin to dawn on her.

Louis might never come to see her again.

That was almost more than she could stand. She waited a couple more days, and a couple more nights, after that thought began haunting her. She slept not at all. And finally, when she could not stand another minute of it, she hitched up a Red River cart, and went, to the agonizing scream of the wheels, out to the mill that Louis Riel's mother operated, on the banks of the small river that the early French fur traders had nostalgically christened the Seine.

Mrs. Riel was there, along with Honore, Louis's twelve-year-old sister. Anna Lee reined in her horse at the gate, jumped down from the cart, and walked into the yard, waving at the two who had become so much like her own family to her.

"Hello, Mrs. Riel."

Mrs. Riel did not answer.

"Hello, Honore, how are you?"

Honore turned without speaking, and went back into the house.

"Is Louis at home, Mrs. Riel?"

Still, Mrs. Riel would not say anything to her. She stared at her without acknowledging her presence, and her mouth was a thin line.

Anna Lee felt tears welling up inside her. "Mrs. Riel, please talk to me!" she cried out. "Please don't do this. It's me, Anna Lee!" I didn't write all those terrible things in the newspaper. I think they're hateful too, just as hateful as you do. I don't want you not to like me because of that. Please, Mrs. Riel, please won't you speak to me?"

Louis appeared in the doorway of the house. Anna Lee saw him, and immediately felt a flood of relief. But that was turned off as quickly as it had started when she saw the black look on his face.

"Louis, can I talk to you?" she asked plaintively. "Will you talk to me, at least? I feel awful. I want to explain . . ."

"We have nothing to say to each other," he told her coldly.

"Louis, this isn't fair . . ."

"I told you we have nothing to say to each other," he said again, snapping off the sentence like a broken key in an old lock.

He went back inside the house, closing the door behind him.

Anna Lee looked desperately at Louis's mother for some form of help, or reassurance, or even pity, knowing that there was no hope of getting it, but . . .

But there was nowhere else to turn. Tough, buxom Julie Riel, with her steel-grey hair and her face heavy with jowls that Anna Lee had seen bubbling and flapping with merriment in days past, was the only other person in sight. And the forbidding coldness in her glance never changed. The jowls were like cast iron now, the thin line of a mouth between them like a sealed fissure. She did not take her hardened eyes off Anna Lee until she was out of the yard, back in her cart, and riding away from the mill.

As she left the Riel place behind her, Anna Lee experienced and knew something that had never been a part of her life before: the cruel, isolating, depersonalizing barrier of racial prejudice. She was being rejected by the man she loved, by a kind old woman whom she had laughed and cried with, to whose stories she had listened spellbound by the hour, by a child whom she had played with and taken care of. Not because of anything inside her, not because she was Anna Lee.

Because she was white.

She knew that people felt that way about *métis*. She knew white girls who did, from the Red River Academy. She knew that Dr. John Schultz did. Worst of all, she knew that her own brother did. But now she knew what it meant.

Mrs. Riel was not even a *métis*. She had been Julie Lajimodière, daughter of the legendary Marie Anne Lajimodière, the first white woman in the Northwest, who had followed her husband a thousand miles further into the wilderness than any white woman had gone before her, who had lived in a buffalo-skin tipi and borne her two daughters in the wilds.

Julie Riel was, herself a white woman who had married a *métis*. How could she now not have compassion for Anna Lee Graham?

Julie Riel was a white woman. Surely she must have more depth of compassion.

Anna Lee heard the words echoing inside her head, and cringed. Did this mean that the same insidious racial prejudice was inside her, too? Was there no escaping from it anywhere?

She did not hear the pounding of hoofbeats over the sound of the Red River cart's screeching, not until she saw a shape out of the corner of her eye and turned around to look over her shoulder.

It was Louis. He was panting from the effort as he pulled even with the cart, and took hold of the bridle to stop the plodding cart horse. For several moments, there was no sound on the prairie but the creaking of the cart as it settled into repose, and the heavy breathing of man and horse as they recomposed themselves after their exertion.

Anna Lee could not say a word. She felt undeserving and ashamed, not worthy of his having come after her, and she bowed her head.

Louis got down from his horse, and looked up at her as she sat on the flat board seat of the Red River cart, twisting her hands in her lap.

He beckoned to her to come down, and she could see that he was as tongue-tied as she was. She could not move. She just kept staring at her hands and twisting them. He beckoned again, and held out one of his huge, rawboned but sensitive hands to her.

This time she managed to unlace her fingers. Placing a palm in his, she allowed herself to be helped down to the ground.

Louis gulped. His Adam's apple bobbed, and his eyes glowed in their dark stillness.

But not a word came out of him. His chest was heaving, and she put the flat of her palm against it to still what she sensed as the wild beating of his heart, as wild and uncontrollable as her own. Then he crushed her to him, and her legs buckled as she held onto him, held him close. He kissed her savagely, painfully, and she gave herself up to the feeling.

The pain meant as much to her now as did the longed-for pleasure of his embrace. She wanted it all, every sensation that he could give to her. She clutched at him as if clutching a dream. She tore at his clothes to touch his body, and she burrowed in to every place that she exposed with wet kisses and searching fingers. She was like an animal, instinctive, ferocious.

He was as wild as she. He made love as if he were fighting, pushing her away as desperately as he pulled her to him. He bruised her with the tightness of his grasp, he drew blood with his teeth in her shoulder, and he entered her with shuddering force that she matched with a wild passion of her own. They made love as if it were for the last time.

12

TALK about Canada acquiring the Northwest had been going on for some time. But it was not until there was really a Canada, a unified Canada, that the talk began to get serious.

By then, the idea had taken on a new urgency. The American Civil War was over; many politicians and military figures from south of the border were turning their eyes toward the unincorporated open territories of the Northwest.

The border had been disputed before—the struggle between Canada and the United States over territory went back into the 18th Century. And throughout the 19th Century, Americans had been talking about invading Canada. An anti-British organization that called itself the Hunters and Chasers of the Eastern Frontier formed lodges all along the border, from Vermont to Michigan, for the express purpose of invading Canada. In 1838, they held a convention in Cleveland and proclaimed a Candian government-in-exile. Later that year, a force of about a thousand men crossed the St. Lawrence River and seized a stone windmill near the town of Prescott, which was held for close to a weak before the garrison was surrounded and the men forced to surrender.

The following year, border disputes in the Northeast led to the Aroostook War of 1839, between Maine and New Brunswick, which ended with no actual casualties, but some real skirmishes, and had both sides arming and raising troops.

Westward migration made for new border conflicts, and the presidential campaign slogan of 1844, "Fifty-four forty or fight," had the United States threatening to go to war if the Canadian-American border was not set, on the Pacific Coast, at a line which was just below the border of Russian-owned Alaska.

And later, after the Civil War, "manifest destiny" became the empire-building cry of American politicians—the United States should extend from sea to shining sea, and from the northern to southern tip of the North American continent. In 1866, a bill was introduced into the United States Senate by Senator Richard Banks, providing for the entry of any or all of the Canadian provinces into the American union.

And in 1867, when American Secretary of State William Henry Seward bought Alaska from the Russians, many Americans laughed at him and called it 'Seward's Folly," but few Canadians were laughing—especially not after Seward announced that one day the whole continent would be a part of the United States of America.

Minnesota, just below Red River, a territory with a population of 6,000 in 1850, was a state with a population of 172,000 ten years later, and by the mid-1860's, emigrants from below the border were forming an "American

Party'' in the Red River settlement, and calling for the area to be annexed by Minnesota.

There had been no Canada until July 1, 1867, no central government to concern itself with issues of Canadian sovereignity. There had been an Upper Canada, which is now the province of Ontario, a Lower Canada—now Quebec— New Brunswick, and Nova Scotia, all separate political entities. Up until that time, when Dr. John Schultz and others talked about the Red River settlement becoming a part of Canada, they had meant Ontario.

But as of July 1, 1867, there was a new Confederation, according to the terms of the British North America Act that brought the four provinces together into the Dominion of Canada, and provided a basis for the kind of westward expansion that the United States had already gotten such a headstart on.

The Dominion had a governor-general appointed by the Crown, a Parliament, and a prime minister. The first prime minister of Canada was Sir John A. MacDonald, who was to remain prime minister for many years, and who would, more than any other man, define the character and scope of the Canadian nation.

Dr. John Schultz, who took a trip to Canada in the spring of 1869, claimed to be an intimate of MacDonald, which was, in fact, not true. His only real connection to MacDonald was that they were both Freemasons, a connection which, by itself, was enough to instill apprehension into the hearts of the Catholic French Canadians and *métis*. They knew very little about the Freemasons—only that they were a secret Protestant fraternal organization, that politically and economically powerful Protestants belonged to it and knew its secret rituals, and that one Mason was likely to have power and leverage with another that no non-Mason could ever expect to compete with.

Schultz did have a friend who was genuinely close to MacDonald, though—William McDougall, Minister of Public Works in MacDonald's first cabinet. McDougall was a tough, shrewd, ambitious man who wanted a lot more for himself than a mere cabinet ministry, and everyone knew it. MacDonald knew it, but MacDonald had the top position in Canada for himself, and no intention of relinquishing it.

Schultz knew it, too—and he knew that MacDougall was becoming obsessed with the need to make his mark quickly. He was forty-five and beginning to worry that life was passing him by, and his opportunities were dwindling. He was precisely the man that Dr. John Schultz wanted to talk to.

Schultz returned to Red River by way of the United States, the same route that he had taken to Ottawa. It was the only way to go: there was no direct passage through Canada.

He went by rail to the end of the line in St. Cloud, Minnesota, and from there by stagecoach to Pembina, the Minnesota border town which was politically part of America, geographically and culturally a part of the Red River settlement.

That meant that Schultz was back where everyone knew who he was—and almost everyone feared, distrusted, and hated him. Schultz's character changed when he reached Pembina. He shed the reserved, polite, British civil servant manner that he used when he dealt with men like McDougall or MacDonald, men to whom he had to give the deference owed to superiors. In its place was the swagger of a colonialist, a freebooter who knew that he could make his own rules. He imperiously summoned a couple of *métis*, had his bags transferred to a Red River cart, and came up the river to Winnipeg.

He met with Charlotte Graham the day after he arrived back.

"Did things go well in Ottawa?" she asked him.

"Well enough," he said. Schultz could scarcely contain his glee, though he tried to keep an imperturbable front. "Annexation is bound to come, and soon. Best of all, it's certain to be under the terms that we want. First, though, we're opening a new store."

"Where?"

"In Oak Point."

"Oak Point? Why on earth?"

Oak Point was near Lake of the Woods, more than fifty miles to the east of Winnipeg. Most of the land between the two outposts was virgin, virtually untravelled forest. There was no road, and the wilderness was all but impassable, except by Indians or the occasional *métis* trapper—all of which Charlotte pointed out.

"There will be one," Schultz said.

"One what?"

"Road. Between Winnipeg and Lake of the Woods. My friend William McDougall, the Minister of Public Works in Ottawa, has authorized it.

"How can he authorize construction of a road from Lake of the Woods to Winnipeg?" Charlotte asked. "He's Minister of Public Works for Canada, and this area isn't part of Canada."

Schultz only smiled; and after a minute, Charlotte smiled too.

"The surveying is going to start almost immediately," Schultz continued. "The road crews will be getting under way soon. Right now, it means that we can still buy out the general store in Oak Point for next to nothing, but as soon as this news gets out, and the activity starts around Lake of the Woods, we'll be sitting on a gold mine. But for the future, it will mean that the door will be opened to easy access from Canada to Red River, and we'll be getting the quality of immigration we've been looking for."

"It does sound good."

"Good? It's perfect! McDougall thinks exactly the way we do, and if he gets what he wants, we get what we want. And he's right there in Ottawa, at MacDonald's right hand. Now what do you say to that?" Schultz puffed himself up with self-importance, and leaned a little closer to her.

"Dr. Schultz, I'd have to say I'm pleased," Charlotte said, moving her body in her chair to twist away from him. "And I'm sure that Mrs. Schultz must be very proud of you, too."

"You know I don't even talk to her about this sort of thing," Schultz said. "She doesn't listen . . . she doesn't understand. It takes a woman like you to truly be able to understand me."

"In a business sense, of course."

"More than that, Mrs. Graham. You know it's more than that. You and I have the kind of understanding that is rare between two people, and we're simply cheating ourselves if we don't—"

By now he was out of his chair, and down on one knee in front of her, clutching her hand in both of his. Charlotte pulled away.

"Dr. Schultz, no! I've told you and told you, it can't work."

"But you've never told me that you didn't find me attractive."

"Dr. Schultz, we're business partners."

It was the only answer that she ever knew how to give

when things got to this point. She was not going to tell him that she did not find him attractive—she needed him too much for that. And while she flirted with him as much as she could bring herself to do so, and although she had done much more for many others she found even less appealing, she could never quite bring herself to tell him the lie that she did find him attractive.

She stood up abruptly, and walked over next to the fireplace.

"Dr. Schultz, I think the idea of taking over the general store in Oak Point is a wonderful idea. You're certainly the cleverest man I've ever known, and we make a great business team. I think I'd like to run the Oak Point store myself."

"You?"

"Yes. I think it would be a good idea, for a number of reasons, for me to get out of this area for a while. It's bound to be a good idea, as far as the other problem we've been having, with . . ."

She coughed genteelly, and nodded toward a daguerrotype of Anna Lee on the mantelpiece.

"Yes, I see what you mean," Schultz acknowledged. "And . . . who knows? I'll certainly be getting over to Oak Point from time to time, and perhaps, if we're farther from my home, and my . . . wife . . ."

"I certainly couldn't make any promises like that, Dr. Schultz," Charlotte said coquettishly.

13

MORE and more, Louis was becoming a mystery to Anna Lee. His moods were so intense, so mercurial. The *métis* community had come to look to him for leadership, as their fears over the threat to their farms and lands mounted.

Louis never wanted to see her publicly any more. He would not say that they had broken off their understanding with each other. But it was hard for Anna Lee to imagine that he was thinking seriously about marrying her, when he was ashamed to let anyone know that he was still having anything to do with her.

The whole community knew, anyway. Anna Lee stood behind the counter of the store in Winnipeg, where everyone passed in and out sooner or later, and she could tell just how much they knew.

Some hot-eyed firebrands would come in, glare at her, and mutter imprecations under their breaths. One or two even went so far as to direct snarling threats at her: "Why don't you get out of here and leave him alone?" Or:

"Louis Riel is a great man, and he must not be brought low. If he compromises his values or his dignity because of your scheming, you'll pay for it!"

Others would look at her with eyes full of sympathy, give her a pat on the hand or the cheek, and say, "Don't worry, dear. He's just a stubborn man, and a proud one. He'll come around."

But for Louis, the deception was real. As far as he was concerned, if he did not acknowledge their relationship, no one else could possibly do so.

So he kept it up. His one confidant, a stocky, taciturn *métis* named Sammy, brought irregular and monosyllabic messages from Louis, never even mentioning him by name: "He wants to see you."

She would go to meet him. But she never knew what it was going to be like. Sometimes he was as loving and passionate as if there were no tomorrow. Then again, he would arrange to meet her, but he would spend the whole tryst with his back to her, ignoring her. Those evenings, she would leave in tears, and he would not even turn around to acknowledge her departure.

But on the evenings when he was loving, and she gave herself up to his love, she left feeling close to tears, too. The other side of him, the rejecting side, was always so close to the surface.

Charlotte waited to announce the move to her family until just a week before they were to go. By then, she and Schultz had made arrangements for someone to take over the Winnipeg store, and the store in Oak Point was nearly ready for them to go to. A *métis* crew, under the direction of a white foreman, was working on renovating and enlarging it.

It was now publicly known that the Dawson Road, named after the engineer who had planned the route, was going to be built. Dr. Schultz, who made the announcement in the *Nor'Wester*, proclaimed editorially that it would be a blessing to the *métis* community, because of the jobs it would bring. Anna Lee hoped it was true. Like everyone else, she had a hard time believing in any promise by Dr. John Schultz to do good for the *métis*.

Certainly the *métis* storekeeper who had sold out the business, just before the revelation about the road project, would not have believed it. Whenever he thought about how much the store had sold for, and how much it became worth less than two weeks later, he cursed himself many times over. But for every time that he cursed himself, he had ten curses for Charlotte Graham and Dr. John Schultz.

James was surly about the move, but he accepted it, especially when it was explained to him that there was an army post there, full of Canadian-English officers and soldiers, and that the road-building crews would be supervised by overseers who were tough, manly, authoritative, and white.

For Anna Lee, it was another story. Charlotte did not even try to soften the blow, nor did she respond to the stricken look on Anna Lee's face when she heard the news. She sat in her rocking chair and gazed at the fireplace, as Anna Lee put her hand to her mouth to stifle a gasp, then managed a cold, "Yes, Ma'am," before she turned and walked quickly out of the room.

She had never felt so alone in her life. She wanted to go somewhere and hide. But that would have availed nothing. Besides, her mother would not have stood for it. She had work to do, and she was expected to do it. So she went out and took her place behind the counter of the store—where everyone in town, it seemed, already knew about the Graham family's plans. Everyone had something to say, from a simple goodbye and good luck to a hissed *good riddance*! Neither response had more effect on her than the other.

But in mid-afternoon, the door opened just far enough to allow a stocky figure to slip through, and Sammy stood there, just inside the doorway, looking as if he did not want to see Anna Lee at all.

For a moment, Anna Lee was not sure if he was even going to come over to the counter and talk to her, or whether he was just going to issue a guttural whisper from across the room, out of earshot, and then slip back out.

But he did walk over to her, and he did whisper so she could hear: "He wants to see you."

"Tell him I'll be there. This evening, after I finish work here at the store."

"No. He wants to see you now."

"Now? That's impossible. I can't leave now. He knows that. Tell him I'll be there at the usual time—when I get out of work here."

"He wants to see you now. Now or not at all," Sammy said impassively.

He did not wait for any more of an answer.

And Anna Lee tried to feel herself caught in a dilemma, but she knew that there was no dilemma. She knew what she was going to do.

She took off her apron, and hung it up on a hook in the back. She got her hat down from another hook, and put it on. She left by the front door of the store, turning the sign around to read CLOSED, and locking up. She put the key in the pocket of her coat.

She knew what she was going to catch from her mother later, because of this. But that was later. Now she had Louis to worry about.

She took a saddle horse, and rode ten miles out of town to the abandoned cabin where she and Louis generally met each other. She was sweaty and uncomfortable as she rode, and bothered by the gnats and midges that buzzed in a cloud around her face, and flew into her eyes and mouth.

Normally, she was used to making this ride in the cool of the evening, not the heat of the afternoon. That was a much more pleasant trip, when the sky was turning rose and pink and purple, and the leaves were turning from green to blue-green to a deep blue-grey. But the heat of the afternoon was the least of what was bothering her.

Louis was not even there when she arrived. She tethered her horse in back of the cabin, and went in to wait for him. She took off her straw hat and put it on the rickety table, and waited. She thought about making a cup of tea, but decided against it. Although she had made tea in this cabin a dozen times before, today she felt like an intruder, and she did not want to touch anything or disturb anything.

She heard hoofbeats outside, and she grabbed her hat off the table, as if she were thinking about making a quick getaway.

She did not bolt for the door, of course. But she was still standing frozen, with her hat in her hand, when Louis came in.

"What are you going to do?" he asked her abruptly.

"What do you mean?"

"What are you going to do? Are you leaving? Are you going to Oak Point or not?"

"I don't know . . . it never occurred to me that I might not. I hadn't even thought about it."

"Well, think about it. You know what it means if you do go."

"Tell me what it means."

"This road is the beginning of the complete destruction of our community."

"That doesn't have anything to do with me. What does

it mean to us if I stay? Are you asking me to stay? Are you asking me to stay with you?''

"I'm telling you that the surveyors are already in Red River, marking out parcels of land to be redivided and sold right out from under their lawful owners. I'm telling you that if you don't stay, you can't get away any longer with saying that it has nothing to do with you, that it's just your mother who is doing all these terrible things. It will be upon your head, just as much as it is on hers, or on the head of Dr. John Schultz."

"Louis, answer me. *Are you asking me to stay here with you?*"

Louis turned his back on her, and walked over to the window. Anna Lee would not follow him. She stood with her arms folded, waiting for his answer.

"Louis, are you asking me to stay with you? Are you asking me to marry you?"

Still, there was no reply. This time, Anna Lee did not wait long. Less than a minute of silence, before she spoke again:

"Louis, I'm going to Oak Point with my mother. Goodbye, Louis."

14

HENRY Sleight was in Oak Point, working on the road. He had been given the job of paymaster for the crew, and had arrived in Oak Point a couple of months ahead of the Grahams.

Anna Lee was glad to see him. It had been over a year since she had spent any time at all with him. Back then, she had been anxious to get away from him, excited by the new prospect of Louis Riel in her life—and bothered, as well, by Henry's arrogance and his high-handed attitude toward her, and toward the people of Red River.

But now, a great deal was changed. She was sure that she had said goodbye to Louis forever. She was heartbroken and lonely in a strange place, and it was reassuring to have a familiar face around.

Henry had changed, too. He seemed to have matured. He was patient and sympathetic where he had once been overbearing and self-centered. He was circumspect about visiting her at first, letting her know that he was available to keep her company, but maintaining his distance until she was ready.

It did not take her long. She needed the company and the friendship too much, and besides, this new Henry Sleight was too appealing to keep out of her life for long.

She needed someone to talk to, as she tried to get her life and her emotions back in balance. She needed a friend. And Henry quickly became that friend.

Charlotte encouraged the friendship. She saw to it that Anna Lee had plenty of free time to spend with Henry. The Graham family were coming up in the world. With the new store, they were starting to live like rich people. Charlotte hired a *métis* couple, Jules and Claire Portecarrère, to work for them: Jules in the store, and Claire as housekeeper.

Anna Lee was a young lady, now, not a shopgirl. She had time to be courted. And Charlotte made sure that she and Henry had plenty of time to be alone.

But Anna Lee was not at all interested in romance at this point in her life. All she wanted was a friend. And Henry, in contrast to his behavior of a couple of years previous, respected her wishes.

Henry's book of poetry had been released, to critical acclaim, and Anna Lee was pleased for him. He had also changed his feelings about the people of the Red River settlement, and confessed his embarrassment over his unkind remarks. He had nothing but respect for the settlers now, *métis* as well as white, he told her, and he was glad to be involved with a project that was bringing work to so many people who really needed it, as well as bringing a road that would connect the eastern and western parts of the settlement, provide means for bringing food in case of famine, medicine in case of plague.

"And a Canadian expansion that will leave the *métis* dispossessed from their lands?" Anna Lee asked.

"What makes you think that? Who have you been talking to?" Henry asked sharply.

There was a moment's awkward silence.

"Oh . . . yes, well . . . of course," Henry said. "I don't mean to say anything against Riel. He's an honest man, and I know that a lot of people respect him. But he's simply not right about what's going to happen. No land is going to be taken away from anybody. All legitimate claims will be upheld. Nobody who has title to his property has anything to fear from the Canadian government."

"I hope not."

"It's as sure as there's a God in Heaven. Just the way Riel was wrong about the local people not wanting this road. You should see how happy they are, from my point of view, as paymaster of the project, looking at all those smiling faces lining up to get paid."

"They're being paid in scrip, aren't they, redeemable at the company store?"

"Why, of course—you wouldn't want them shopping anywhere else, would you? You've got the best merchandise, and the fairest prices. They'd just get cheated and taken advantage of, if they got real money and could take it around just anywhere. These people are like children, take my word for it. I see too many of them not to know that."

"Well . . . I suppose so."

She was not sure of his logic. But she was not completely sure how much she cared any more, either. Louis Riel could have had her by his side if he had wanted, but he had turned her down. His causes were not her causes any longer.

That fall, in the company of her mother, her brother, and Henry Sleight, Anna Lee visited Ottawa. She had never seen anything so grand, or so modern, as the confederation's capital city. People dressed for every day in the clothes that Anna Lee would have thought dressy even for Sunday out in Red River. She felt ragged and woebegone even in the Sunday dress she had worn to town, until they took her to an elegant store and bought her a whole new wardrobe.

She saw the sights of Ottawa, rode in a streetcar, went to the theater. She had never been to a theatrical performance before, but she had read the play they were doing—Shakespeare's *Measure for Measure*. She thought it was interesting, but perhaps not as interesting as the way she had already played it out, many times, in her imagination. One or two of the actors on stage portrayed the characters almost as well as she had portrayed them in her head, and the others did not. She found the costumes to be the best part of the show, the one part that was beyond what she could have imagined.

She went to a ball, too. *That* was something that lived up to all of her expectations.

More than she had ever imagined. Much, much more. Not even vaguely like the dances back in Red River, with the fiddle and guitar and grizzly old step caller.

It began with the ball gown that she had bought for the occasion—silk and brocade, with a waistline stitched and fitted so that it fit exactly to her waist and ribcage; with both shoulders bare, and a broad bare V across her chest.

''Mademoiselle has such . . . unusual skin,'' said the salesgirl who helped her choose it. Anna Lee knew what she meant by that. Her face and neck were tanned from the prairie sun. The rest of her body—her shoulders, her chest and the swelling tops of her breasts—were never touched by the sun. They were snowy white. Anna Lee wondered if it would be a problem, but she decided that these people, who were the cosmopolitan Canadians, were selling her the gown, and they must know what they were doing. She decided not to worry about it.

In fact, she was scarcely thinking about herself at all. The gown was the focus of her attention. She thought that it was so beautiful, so brilliant, so striking, that if she wore it, she would be safe. People would look only at it, and not at her.

It had not occurred to her until she walked into the ballroom, on Henry Sleight's arm, that every other woman would also be wearing a sumptuous gown. That discovery might have intimidated her, but it did not. She was still riding a crest of exhilaration, and she sparkled with it like the highlights of sun off a clear northwestern lake at sunset.

She was eighteen years old, and within a space that could be measured in days, she had gone from the frontier wilderness to the summit of Canadian society.

Or so it seemed to her. Over a period of a couple of years her mother, through her association with Dr. John Schultz, had become wealthy, but Anna Lee had not even realized it until they had gone to Oak Point. Even then, it had meant little to her, except that she no longer had to work behind the counter of the store. It was only the suddenly buying beautiful clothes, suddenly staying in a fine hotel, that had made it sink in to her. Like Cinderella, in the twinkling of an eye, with the wave of a wand, she was rich and beautiful.

Anna Lee had never even dreamed about a moment like this. Her plans and dreams and hopes for the future had all centered around Louis Riel. And she honestly did not know, even here in Ottawa with all her beautiful new clothes, how completely she had left those other dreams behind her.

So there was really no reason at all for her to feel tense and nervous at the ball. It was too unreal for her. It was a fantasy come true that had never been her fantasy. It was a gown for people to admire that they said was hers, but it had only been hers for a matter of hours, and she as yet felt no personal connection to it, except insofar as she admired it also.

It was a game with no stakes, and so she played it lightly, easily—and, she was soon to discover, brilliantly. She had no trouble talking to anybody, and there was no shortage of people for her to talk to.

All of them were men. They clustered around, and asked her one question after another just to hear her talk. They asked her what her reactions were to Ottawa, and they asked her questions about life on the frontier.

She answered everything frankly and fully. Unlike other belles from the provinces, the daughters of Army officers and high officials of the Hudson's Bay Company, she did not try to disguise or gloss over her origins at all, nor did she try to pretend to an urbanity that she did not have; and it made her irresistible.

Everyone wanted to dance with her, too. Anna Lee loved the dancing. There was an orchestra right there in the room, not just a couple of squeaky fiddles, but over a dozen men in impeccable evening attire, playing violins and a cello and a bassoon and even a grand piano, all of them in tune.

The music was not as lively as it had been for the dances in Red River, but it was beautiful. And the men did not dance as well as the partners who had squired her on the frontier. But they were handsome, and they smelled good, and they were exciting in their own way.

It was easy for Anna Lee to respond to that excitement. She did not know the dances at first, but they were easy to learn, and then she put herself into them in the same open, uninhibited manner that she had put herself into conversation.

She was too young and beautiful and graceful to be

vulgar. She was just herself. But every man who danced with her, who felt the squeeze of her hand, the brush of her cheek or her arm, found himself glowing like an ember in a country fireplace for the rest of the evening.

Late in the evening, she found herself in the company of two older men. Her mother introduced her.

Charlotte Graham made it clear from the anxious tightness to her smile, the unnatural lilt to her voice, that she was very much impressed by both of these gentlemen, and that she wanted Anna Lee to make a good impression on them.

Anna Lee disregarded her mother's anxiety. She did not know who these two middle-aged gentlemen were, but by this point in the evening, she was hardly worried about her ability to charm anyone. She took that as a given, and she was starting to look with a critical, discerning eye on the people she met.

She liked one of the gentlemen, the older one. He was in his fifties, she guessed, but still vigorous. He was very much a man of the city, but he had a tough, resourceful quality to him that Anna Lee recognized and responded to immediately. His name was Sir John A. MacDonald.

"It's a pleasure to meet you, my dear," MacDonald said. "My advance scouts from among the young men tell me that you are quite the most refreshing new face to arrive in Ottawa that anyone can remember."

"Thank you, Mr. MacDonald," Anna Lee said. "It's a pleasure to meet you, too. Are you from the West, by any chance?"

"I'm afraid not, my dear. I've only fleetingly been as far as western Ontario, and even on those occasions, I was hardly roughing it. Do I look like a Westerner to you?"

"Well, no," Anna Lee conceded. "But you look like the sort of man who could hold his own in the West, if he had to. I'd guess that you could hold your own anywhere, Mr. MacDonald."

MacDonald gave a hearty laugh. "Thank you, my dear," he said. "I take that as a high compliment."

"What about me?" asked the other gentleman, thrusting his chin and shoulders forward in a gesture that was supposed to be hearty and aggressive, but succeeded only in looking petulant.

He was the one whom Anna Lee did not like, from the moment she laid eyes on him. He had been introduced to her as William McDougall.

MacDonald had the steely toughness Anna Lee had seen in the best of the frontiersmen, combined with other qualities which were new to her, but she recognized them instinctively. There was a delicacy around his eyes, and an ironic play to his lips, that indicated a precision of perception and a depth of understanding that were formidable.

Anna Lee found it intriguing and a little unnerving at the same time. She could not expect to put anything over on this man. She doubted very much if she could keep any secret from him, if he wanted to find it out.

When she was told, later, that he was the most powerful man in Canada, the information did not come as a surprise to her.

McDougall, on the other hand, was a whiner. That was the first thing Anna Lee noticed about him, and the most important fact about him, she decided quickly. He was intelligent, but he would not use his intelligence to make the best decisions. He was interested in power, excited by power, he probably even understood a lot about power and how to get the trappings of it; but he would never be a powerful man. He was a weakling.

"What about me?" William McDougall repeated peevishly. "I'm the one you should be saying would get along well on the frontier."

"Oh, there's no question about it, Mr. McDougall," Charlotte said with forced enthusiasm. She shot Anna Lee a look, the meaning of which was clear: You'd better say the same thing, and sound like you mean it.

Anna Lee said nothing. There is no way in the world that this man could get by on the frontier, she thought. Maybe here, where he understands the rules. But out there, every weakness he has would be exposed.

MacDonald caught her eye, and she knew that he knew what she was thinking. His mouth wrinkled in ironic sympathy as his eyes held hers.

"Mr. McDougall has just been named lieutenant governor of all of the territory between Lake of the Woods and the Rocky Mountains," he said.

"Congratulations, Mr. McDougall," Anna Lee said coolly.

"Would you dance with an old man, Miss Graham?" MacDonald asked her.

"I'd be honored, Mr. MacDonald."

"You do me the honor, Miss Graham. I'll count on these old legs to get from one end of a waltz to the other. And I shall take full advantage of the one tangible and unarguable privelege of my rank that I have yet discovered: no one will dare to cut in on us."

"You don't care for Mr. McDougall a great deal, do you, my dear?" MacDonald asked her.

Trying to be tactful, she did not reply.

"No matter. I can see you're too much of the diplomat already, after only a few short days in Ottawa, to answer so blunt a question. Well, I can't stand him myself. It's a constant source of amazement to me that a man with so much intelligence and ability should be so devoid of real judgement, tact, and common sense—and so unaware that he is. He has the credentials to become lieutenant governor of the Northwest, certainly. But that's not the reason why I agreed to give him the appointment. The real reason is simply that I can't stand to have him around."

Anna Lee giggled. "But, Mr. MacDonald," she asked, "how can you appoint a lieutenant governor to a territory that's not part of Canada?"

She was not sure she wanted to have asked that question. It brought memories of Louis back into her head, and suddenly made her less glad that she was there.

MacDonald sensed it, and looked down into her eyes. "Of course, his appointment remains pending the sale of the territory from the Hudson's Bay Company to the Dominion of Canada," he said. "But you didn't come to Ottawa to spend all your time talking about the Northwest, did you? Tell me, how are you enjoying yourself here? Could you imagine yourself moving to Ottawa . . . living here?"

"Oh, I . . . I don't know. I never thought about it."

"Well, if you ever do think about it, Ottawa will be the richer for it, just as the Red River settlement will be the worse for William McDougall. If he drives you back here, out of sheer boredom with his pomposity, it will be a most worthwhile exchange."

"Oh, Mr. MacDonald, you're making fun of me."

"Not at all. You'd do well in Ottawa. You're bright and attractive, and you could hold your own with anyone. I, for one, would be delighted to see you here. And if I were twenty years younger, and less happily married—as yet unmarried, I mean to say, of course—I should be particularly happy to see you here."

Henry Sleight came to reclaim Anna Lee for the last dance. It was reassuring to see him. The excitement of the evening, especially the company of Sir John MacDonald, was getting too much for her, and she relaxed gratefully in

Henry's arms, and afterwards leaned her head against his shoulder contentedly on the ride home.

He kissed her hand at the door.

"Thank you, Henry," she said. "It was a wonderful evening. I'll never forget it."

"There will be more like it," he said. "I'll give you more. I'll give you anything you'll let me, Anna Lee."

"Thank you, Henry," she said again. "We'll see."

And she closed the door quickly.

Charlotte wanted Anna Lee to stay up, so that she could ask her all about her evening, but Anna Lee demurred, saying that she was too tired, and had to get right to bed. She knew that her mother was angry, but she would not be swayed.

Back in her room, Anna Lee thought about her mother. This was the first time that Charlotte had ever seemed to want an exchange of mother-daughter confidences.

In a way, it was tempting. Anna Lee tried to imagine herself sitting down with Charlotte in the parlor of their hotel suite, and talking to her openly, woman to woman. She would tell her about the passion and confusion that she had lived with ever since she met Louis Riel. She would ask her mother if she had ever been in love, when she was young. If she had ever slipped out to meet a man. If she knew what it was like to tremble with desire, to want to hold someone you loved so tightly that you could make yourself believe that you could hold him inside you forever, and he would never leave you.

She could not imagine that her mother had ever felt any such thing. She had never known Charlotte to be interested in anything except business. She could not imagine her making love, or thinking about romance.

But if she could . . .

She would try to explain what it was like to be swept

away with excitement that made her feel warm and flushed in every pore of her body, and feeling guilty about it, because it felt like betraying her lover. Even though he had already betrayed her by casting her aside. She would have asked her mother if it was all right for her to enjoy herself, to like the beauty and the luxury and the attention that were suddenly being showered on her.

And she would ask her what it meant to feel comfortable with a man like Henry Sleight. Was that a different kind of love, and was she just being difficult by not seeing it that way? Or could it turn into love, after a while? She needed to know.

But there was no point in talking to Charlotte about any of that. All her mother would ever want to know was if she had made any connections which would help the family business.

Family business . . . what family? She had always felt like an outsider. No wonder it was so easy for her to identify with Cinderella in her new ball gown, and why she thought of the whole evening as so unreal. She *was* Cinderella, working in the store all day, living on rejection and coldness. And no Prince Charming at the ball, either.

As her euphoric mood completely crumpled, and she threw herself down on the bed, weeping bitterly, an image from her childhood sprang into her mind: sitting wrapped up in a blanket, her arm in a sling, shivering in front of a fire, and hearing her little brother hiss across at her:

"She saved me first."

She was shivering again, cold and lonely. She took off her ball gown, folded it, and laid it across the oak chest in her room. She put on a warm flannel nightgown, and got into bed.

With drowsiness, the good memories started to come back, and she began to lull herself to sleep with the sound of the music, the feel of the soft hands of gentlemen, the shining glow of attentive faces. And as she relaxed, even the thought of sharing all those happy moments with her mother seemed more pleasant.

She was not sure if she had actually been to sleep, or how late it was. She knew that the door had opened and closed, and that there was someone else in the room with her.

"Mother . . .?" But there was no answer.

She sat up in bed, and lit the candle. The wick blazed up when she touched the match to it, and for a moment all she could see was a glow before her eyes. Then it settled down into a flicker, and her eyes grew accustomed to it, and she could see, by the doorway, her brother James. He was in his nightshirt too, standing with his arms folded, glowering at her.

"Oh, it's you," she said. "What are you doing here? I'm trying to sleep. I'll tell you all about it in the morning."

He did not reply. He just kept glowering at her.

"Well, go on!" she said crossly. "I want to go to sleep. What's the matter with you, anyway?"

"I don't see why they let you go and not me," he said. "What's that supposed to mean? What do they think I am—not good enough, or something?"

"What are you talking about?" she asked. "You're too young. You're just a child. They don't let children go to fancy balls like that. It's not like the dances back in Red River."

"Don't tell me I should be back in Red River," he said. "I'm just as good as you."

"James, please. You're being ridiculous."

"If I told them everything about you that I know about you, they'd find out whether you were good enough to have all those fancy people making a big fuss over you,'' he said. ''See if they wouldn't.''

''You don't know anything about me.''

''I know you think you're better than me, but you're not. I know you're nothing but a *whore*!''

He spoke the word with the careful pronunciation of someone who has just learned it.

''You get out of here and leave me alone!''

''I'll bet you Mama knows what kind of person you are.''

''Have you told her . . .?''

James snickered. ''Scared you, didn't I? I don't have to tell her. She may not know as much as I know, but she knows you're no good. That's why she loves me best. She wouldn't love me best if she didn't know that I was just as white as she is. That proves it, doesn't it? That proves that Papa was really my father, and Mama really loves me best.''

''James, I'm going to scream if you don't get out of here. You're talking nonsense.''

''Nonsense, is it? You think it's nonsense? Well, it's not, it's true! It's all true! I'm the one who should be going to fancy balls, not you, and I will, too! This is what you should be!''

James snatched up Anna Lee's ball gown from the top of the dresser, and before she could make a move to stop him, he had ripped the front, from bodice to waist.

Anna Lee leaped out of bed, but then she stopped. She realized that she was afraid to approach him.

''You're crazy! What do you think you're doing?''

''Just what you deserve! Just what you've got coming to you!''

He dropped the gown at his feet. Slowly, as she stood transfixed, he lifted the hem of his nightshirt.

By the flickering candlelight, his penis seemed darker than the rest of his body. And large, as fully developed as a grown man's. He held it between the thumb and first two fingers of his right hand, aimed it, and urinated directly on the torn gown.

15

ALL the provisions of the deal had been worked out by autumn of 1869, and the Hudson's Bay Company, in return for the payment of 300,000 pounds in cash agreed to surrender all of its land holdings to the British government. Great Britain would then transfer the land to the Dominion of Canada, as soon as Canada was ready to take effective possession.

And the surveyors were out in force, under the command of Lieutenant Colonel John Stoughton Dennis, Surveyor of Public Lands of the Northwest, appointed by the Ministry of Public Works. They were supposed to be doing nothing but surveying land for the road; but they seemed, to anyone who was paying any attention at all, to be doing much more than that. To begin with, they started going off the path of the roadway, and surveying all the desirable areas of land that were not actually claimed by the settlers. And the next thing that anyone knew, they were staking out their own claims on that land.

Anna Lee Graham was not one of those who was paying any attention at all. From the time that they returned from Ottawa, she managed to spend almost all her time with Henry Sleight, talking about everything under the sun except the controversies that swirled around the Red River settlement.

By the second week in October, he asked her to marry him. And she accepted.

She still did not know if she loved him. But she knew that she felt comfortable with him. And that she had to get away from home.

But the survey was continuing nonetheless. Dennis was using the American system of survey, dividing the land into squared areas of 640 acres apiece. None of the existing farms in Red River fitted into that pattern. They were laid out in narrow strips, so as to give every farmer some of the river frontage that was so necessary to a farm in the area.

The Red River farms were eight to fifteen chains wide, using the local system of measurement. A chain was sixty-six feet. They were two to four miles deep, and they belonged to the Scottish families whom Lord Selkirk had brought in, or to the *métis*—Hudson's Bay Company employees who had applied to Selkirk, and later, to the company, for land grants. They all had legal title to their lands, but few of them had written deeds to prove it.

No one was sure what the Canadians had in mind. And few people were made to feel easier by the disclosure of the fact that the name which was turning up most commonly on the new land claims was that of Dr. John Schultz.

On October 11, a farmer named Andre Nault found a group of surveyors on his property. He went to find out what was going on, but nobody on the surveying crew spoke French, and all they could do was to shrug at Nault's angry gesticulations.

Nault went off to get outside help. Dennis called his foreman.

"Mike, go into town and get us someone who can speak French. Get the paymaster, Sleight. He knows enough to get by. And he can deal with these people. He's lived here for a while."

Andre Nault had gone to find someone who could speak English. When Mike the foreman got back with Henry Sleight, there was no one there for Sleight to talk to but Colonel Dennis.

"What's the problem, Colonel?"

"That's what I brought you here to find out."

"Are you surveying on the fellow's land?"

"How the hell should I know, Sleight? I'm a surveyor, not a Chinese puzzle expert. Who can figure out what's somebody's land and what's not around here? Not me, that's for damn sure. Tell them to have real property boundaries like anyone else, and I'll stay the hell off them. What the hell else do you expect a man to do?"

Three riders approached from the direction of the river. From a distance, Henry Sleight could tell that two of them were *métis*, from the splashes of bright color: one wore a red flannel shirt, the other a red sash and bandana.

The third was all dressed in somber black; but as they drew near, Sleight recognized him as a *métis*, too.

It was Louis Riel.

Riel's horse was two paces in the lead, and he cantered up and pulled to a stop in front of the surveying party, with the others right behind him.

He sat in the saddle for several moments, staring down at Sleight. Sleight could feel the hot breath of Riel's horse's nostrils.

"Hello, Riel," he finally said.

Reil still said nothing. Finally, he swung down from his horse. Resting the reins on the ground, he walked over between two of the surveyors, who were still working their equipment. His foot lashed out, and the stake flew out of the closest surveyor's hands. Riel then stepped down hard on the chain, and held it under his foot.

One member of the crew picked up a shotgun, another a pickaxe. Riel, unarmed, stood his ground. Nault and the other *métis* stepped up behind him. They, too, were unarmed.

Riel kept his eyes on Sleight.

"What are you doing here?" he demanded. "Does Dr. John Schultz think he already owns M. Nault's property, that he sends his lackey to keep watch over it?"

"I just came as an interpreter, Riel. Nobody here understood the problem. They're just doing a job, and perhaps they strayed off course. You know as well as I do that none of this land has ever been properly surveyed, and it's easy to make a mistake. If this is M. Nault's land, then Colonel Dennis apologizes, and he'll be glad to leave."

"Just doing a job, is it? And who are they doing this job for?"

"I beg your pardon?"

"I said who are they working for? The Hudson's Bay Company?"

"You know damn well that they're working for the government of Canada."

"Don't blaspheme in front of me. There is no government of Canada in the Red River settlement."

"The Hudson's Bay Company agrees in principle with what the government of Canada is doing."

"I know for a fact that the Hudson's Bay Company was not even consulted on the building of this road, much less the surveying."

"Look here, Riel," Sleight said, throwing out his hands.

"I understand what you're saying. But don't think everyone is against you. There are a lot of us in the territory who feel that annexation can benefit *all* the people of Red River, and who will do everything in their power to insure that the rights of the existing settlers will be protected."

Nault tugged at Riel's sleeve. *"Ils violent ma propriétéencore,"* he said.

The crew had not moved since this exchange began. The man with the shotgun and the man with the pickaxe continued to hold them at the ready. The others stood at their posts, waiting for some signal as to what they should do. Riel lifted his foot off the chain.

"Get them out of here," he said to Sleight.

Sleight nodded to Dennis. "It appears that it's the gentleman's farm," he said. "I'd suggest you suspend work here until it's proven otherwise."

Dennis gave the order. "All right men. Pick up your gear."

Sleight stood his ground, opposite Riel, until the surveying equipment was loaded back onto the wagon, and the crew was on its way. Then he bowed stiffly to Riel, and mounted his own horse.

"Mr. Sleight!" Riel called to him as he was turning to go.

"Yes, M. Riel?"

"I understand that you have become engaged to be married. Congratulations."

William McDougall left Ottawa that same week, with an entourage, and an itinerary that took them down to America, across to St. Cloud Minnesota, and up to the border crossing at Pembina.

"You know you've no official standing there until legal authority over the settlement is transferred to Canada on December 1," MacDonald told him.

"I know, Sir John," blustered McDougall. "I merely intend to let the natives know who I am, and to establish myself in the community."

"Well, stay out of trouble."

"I hardly expect any trouble, Sir John. Dr. Schultz assures me that the entire community is eagerly awaiting our presence."

Sleight went to see Dr. John Schultz, and caught him in his real estate office.

"Bit of trouble yesterday, John," he said.

"How's that?"

"Dennis's surveying crew ended up in a half-breed's back yard, and very nearly caused an incident."

"Careless of him." Schultz did not seem perturbed by the report.

"I was called upon to interpret for Dennis, who didn't seem to know what was going on. Turned out not to be necessary, because the half-breed went out for reinforcements too, and came back with this fellow Riel, who speaks English, of course. I talked with him."

Schultz snorted. He did not look pleased at the mention of Riel's name.

"I told Riel that it was a mistake, and that we had no intention of disturbing existing farms."

"Good idea."

"I just want to know if I was telling the truth. I mean, I didn't set my name down on a binding oath, or anything, but . . ."

"Anyone who has a legitimate claim to his land will see that claim honored. That does not include every nomadic half-breed who's squatting on good farmland half the year while he goes out hunting buffalo—or other half-breeds' squaws, or whatever he takes it into his head to go hunting after."

"That may be a hard distinction to draw."

"Don't you worry about it. We'll figure it out. And we'll make sure that we get ours. That's what counts, isn't it?"

"Yes, sir. That's what counts."

16

HENRY Sleight went for dinner at the Grahams' home that evening, still preoccupied. He was able to disguise it during the meal, as Charlotte kept up a conversational monologue that was equal parts gossip, complaint, and economic report. James was sullen, and ate quickly. He did not enter into the conversation, but for Sleight, the teenager's mere presence was enough to discourage him from speaking what was on his mind, especially when it came to his own new-found doubts about the treatment of the *métis*. James's virulent racism was well known.

Later, Henry and Anna Lee sat in the parlor together.

"You're very quiet tonight, Henry," Anna Lee said.

"Something happened this afternoon, and I'm trying to figure out how I feel about it."

"Yes?"

"It had to do with a confrontation between Colonel Dennis' road crew and a group of *métis*. It was—"

Anna Lee's face had turned stiff, with the corners of her mouth frozen in a downward turn.

"I don't think I want to hear about it, Henry."

"Nothing bad happened, dearest. It was settled peacefully. It just made me wonder . . ."

"Henry, I mean it. I'm sorry. You've been very sympathetic to me, and you've always listened to me when I had something I needed to talk about. But I don't want to hear about this. I don't want to know about *métis* and Canadians and who's right or wrong."

Henry could see that she really meant it. More than that, it was urgently important to her.

"All right, then," he said. He searched for some new conversational thread, but nothing occurred to him. He got up to stir the fire, and the sparks fell from the half-burned log in a softly glowing shower.

Wishing he could so easily stir loose from himself the same kind of glowing, free-falling sparks of light, Henry looked down into the fire for a few moments longer. Then he returned, and sat down by Anna Lee again.

"Henry, after we're married, could we move away from here? Could we live in Ottawa?"

"Are you serious, dearest?" Henry asked her, surprised. "Is that really what you want?"

"Yes. I've been thinking about it a lot. I know you came out here to build a career, but . . . it's not a good place. I know bad things are going to happen here—I feel it. And I want to get away—I really do. I want it more than anything!"

"All right, dearest," Henry said. "I'll see what I can do."

She put her hand into his. He held it, and they stared into the fire together.

17

WILLIAM McDougall's party enjoyed the trip out. It was paid for by the Canadian government. They had three private railroad cars at their disposal, including a bar where a liveried bartender dispensed champagne, brandy, and the finest of Scotch whiskeys. They stopped the train for an afternoon of grouse shooting. McDougall held interviews with the press in St. Paul, in which he announced grandly that Canada was on the threshold of her destiny, a destiny that would soon match or overshadow that of the United States. He did not shrink from the suggestion that William McDougall was the key to that destiny.

At St. Cloud, the governor's baggage, including his personal luggage, furniture, government files, and several crates containing three hundred Enfield rifles, were transferred into a wagon train of sixty separate wagons and carts, loaded and driven by *métis* cart drivers, for the trip to Pembina.

They started on the trail to Pembina on October 11. It was a glorious Indian summer in the Northwest that October, or, as the locals called it, the "little summer of St. Luke." Evenings were frosty, and mornings might see a little skin of ice on the surfaces of the ponds they passed, especially by the end of their trip, but middays were warm, sunny, and ablaze with color. The skies were full of migrating birds, mallards, Canada geese, teal and swans, and for the early morning risers, the duck hunting was excellent.

Up and down the trail, a scattering of *métis* horsemen passed them from time to time. Some of them stopped briefly to talk to the carters, but they were quickly shooed away so as not to distract the men from their work.

The trip took two and a half weeks. McDougall's party arrived in Pembina on October 30, and made ready to cross the border into the British territory that would soon be part of Canada.

McDougall sent a couple of his men over for the formality of reporting to the American border customs house, before the group proceeded across the border.

When they came back one of the men handed McDougall a note. "This was left for you at the customs house, sir," he said.

McDougall tore it open perfunctorily, and his eyes widened in outrage as he read it:

Sir,
The National Committee of the Métis *at Red River orders Mr. William McDougall not to enter the territory of the Northwest without special permission of this committee.*

Signed,
LOUIS RIEL, Secretary

"Who gave you this?" McDougall demanded.

"A group of men over at the customs house, sir. They looked like Indians—I believe they must have been half-breeds, sir."

"Tell them . . . never mind. I'll go and speak to them myself."

McDougall thundered across to the customs house. He ignored the customs inspectors, who were as pointedly ignoring him, and spoke to the two *métis* couriers.

"What's the meaning of this? You ignorant savages, you've got no right to threaten me! I'm a representative of the government!"

"That's not true, Mr. McDougall."

"It's as good as true. I was told . . . where is the welcoming committee that was supposed to come and meet me at the border?"

"Reckon we're it."

"Don't play games with me. Have you forcibly waylaid them? I know I was expected, and the people of Red River are ready to welcome me as their new governor. Dr. Schultz assured me of it."

The American border guards let out a snicker, and McDougall whirled on them.

"I don't need any insolence out of you. And as for you—" he turned back to the *métis*—"this is what I think of your seditious garbage."

He tore the proclamation in half, crumpled it, and threw it in a corner of the border station.

"I have every intention of entering Canada, and entering Canada today. I need permission from no one except the honorable Sir John MacDonald—certainly not from a bunch of cretinous savages."

McDougall went back to the head of the wagon train.

"We're going on," he said. "We cross the border into Canada at once."

* * *

They put up at an abandoned Hudson's Bay Company trading post a few miles north of Pembina. McDougall pounded the ground officiously with his hunting rifle, when he stepped down from his wagon.

"Canada," he said. "And no blasted half-breeds bothering us, either."

"What do we do now,sir?"

"Uh . . . well . . . nothing for the present," McDougall harrumphed. "We'll stay here for the evening, and wait. I fully expect a welcoming party of loyal Red River citizens to be here in the morning, and to escort us to Winnipeg in the style we have a right to expect. I fully expect that we will receive word from Dr. Schultz, perhaps as early as this evening."

No official word from Dr. Schultz, or anyone else, arrived that evening. One visitor from the Red River settlement did make the trip down to the border, however, to pay a call on McDougall.

"Henry Sleight, sir," the visitor introduced himself. "We met in Ottawa."

"Yes, yes, pleased to see you, Sleight," rumbled McDougall, looking at him without recognition. "What can I do for you?"

"I took it upon myself to come down and see you, sir. I missed you at Pembina, but I heard you'd had some trouble at the border."

"Nothing but a lot of silly impudence by a bunch of dissatisfied half-breeds with whom I'll deal as soon as I get to Winnipeg," McDougall said. "When is the official greeting committee going to arrive?"

"I'm afraid that between myself and the *métis* committee, that's all there is, sir," Sleight said. "I came to warn you that the message you received from those men at the border may be more a reflection of the majority sentiment in the territory than you were led to believe."

"Nonsense. What do you mean? Dr. Schultz—"

"Dr. Schultz is my friend, sir, and I wouldn't speak against him. But I believe that he's been misunderstood—just as your presence may be misunderstood—by a rather large segment of the community. They're not—I firmly believe that they're not against annexation by Canada; they just don't know exactly what it means, and they're looking for certain guarantees that their property rights will be safeguarded. I don't believe that they'll harm you. But I am afraid you can't expect that they will be glad to see you."

"Nonsense! All stuff and nonsense," McDougall harrumphed. "You go back and tell Schultz . . . tell the Hudson's Bay Company governor . . . tell someone that I damn well expect an escort up from the border, and I want it here tomorrow!"

There was, in fact, an escort at McDougall's door the next day. It was an armed patrol of fourteen *métis*, with a message for the Canadians:

"You and your company are to leave the Red River territory by nine o'clock this morning."

"I'll have you arrested for this," McDougall said. "I'll see you all hanged. When I report this to the government—"

"There is no government," Ambroise Lépine, the patrol leader, told him. "Canada has no official status here. And you've stripped the Hudson's Bay Company of authority so completely that none of their officials care what happens here any more. They're not governing. There's no one you can report to . . . except the National Committee of the *Métis*, to which you may apply for special permission to enter the territory."

"I'll see you in hell, first!"

They were back outside the border station at Pembina.

"Without permission, you may not cross the border again," Lépine told him. The patrol rode off and left him, as the amused border guards came out of their shack to watch the Canadian dignitary turn red and then purple with rage.

Lépine reported back to Riel that afternoon.

"Does McDougall have troops?" Riel asked.

"Troops? No. A dozen stuffed shirts with fowling pieces. But he does have a good-sized arsenal of guns—three hundred Enfield rifles, my spies tell me. Enough to arm Dennis's surveying teams and whatever mercenaries he can hire around here, until he can bring in more men from Canada. And he's not going to negotiate with us while there's any alternative."

"Well, somebody has to. MacDonald, or somebody from the Canadian government. And they're not going to have to if McDougall and Dennis and Schultz take control of the territory."

"McDougall's safely south of the border."

"Dennis isn't. And as long as . . ."

Fort Garry, in downtown Winnipeg where the Assiniboine and Red Rivers come together, was a sturdily built fort, still maintained and supplied by the Hudson's Bay Company, although staffed by only a skeleton crew these days. It would be an important base of operations for anyone who wanted control of the Red River settlement, both tactically and symbolically.

And on November 2, Louis Riel, at the head of a force of 120 armed *métis*, entered Fort Garry.

William Cowan, the Hudson's Bay Company representative in charge of the fort, came out to meet them.

"What do you want here, with all these armed men?" he asked Riel.

"We have come to guard the fort."

"Against whom?"

"Against a danger which I have reason to believe threatens it. That is all I can explain to you at the present. We do not want to be violent, and will respect all persons and all property belonging to the Hudson's Bay Company."

Cowan looked at the men behind Riel. He knew most of them. They were good company men, the backbone of the Red River settlement. And Riel's character and reputation was known to everyone in the settlement.

"Come in, then," said Cowan. "We won't try to stop you."

18

NOBODY was about to stop Louis Riel. McDougall's only allies were the crowd around Dr. John Schultz, and they represented a very small minority of the Red River populace. McDougall himself had not even any legal power, much less force of arms. And the Hudson's Bay Company had withdrawn from the picture. The Hudson's Bay Company's territorial governor, William MacTavish, was sick and dying, and in any case, he had been left out of the negotiations between Canada, Britain, and the Hudson's Bay Company's main offices.

The settlers of Red River did not necessarily approve of what looked like an insurrection, but all of them, even the Scottish farmers, were worried about the land grab that appeared to be shaping up under the rule of McDougall and Dennis, so no one was particularly opposed to Riel.

McDougall sent a message to MacDonald in Ottawa: "A small band of troublemakers has prevented me, temporarily, from entering the country. Dr. Schultz assures me, however, that the majority of the populace is still loyal. On December 1, when the Red River settlement officially becomes a part of Canada, I will once again cross the border and proclaim my governorship of the territory, at which point the rabble that presently occupies Fort Garry can be arrested and tried for treason.

"Meanwhile, I continue to wait in this primitive and squalid little border town, forced to bear up under the gibes and insults of American border guards and these filthy, illiterate half-breeds alike. This is a country that has a few lessons to learn, and I assure you, Sir John, I am the man to teach them."

MacDonald got the message on November 26, the same day that he had wired the British Colonial Office: "Canada cannot accept Northwest until peaceable provision can be given. We hereby advise the Colonial Office, and the Hudson's Bay Company, to delay issue of the proclamation until this matter is settled."

After he read McDougall's letter, the prime minister called in his secretary, and began to dictate a reply.

" 'My Dear McDougall: You impossibly inept fool and bungler, what the hell can you possibly be thinking of? Even for you, this is . . .'

"No, I can't say that, unfortunately. Start again. 'You speak of crossing the line and being sworn in the moment you receive official notice of the transfer of the Territory. Now, it occurs to us that that step cannot well be taken. You ought not to swear that you will perform duties that you are, by action of the insurgents, prevented from performing.

" 'By assuming the government, you relieve the Hudson's Bay Company authorities from all responsibility in the matter. As things stand they are responsible for the peace and good government of the country, and ought to be held to that responsibility until they are in position to give peaceable possession.

" 'A proclamation, such as you suggest, calling upon the people, in your capacity as Lieutenant Governor, to unite to support the law, and calling upon the insurgents to disperse, would be very well if it were sure to be obeyed. If, however, it were disobeyed, your weakness and inability to enforce the authority of the Dominion would be painfully exhibited, not only to the people of Red River, but to the people and Government of the United States, who, as you know, also have an interest in the Red River territory.

" 'An assumption of the government by you, of course, puts an end to that of the Hudson's Bay Company's authorities, and Governor Mactavish and his council would be deprived of even the legal right to interfere. There would then be, if you were not admitted into the country, no legal government existing and anarchy must follow. In such a case, no matter how the anarchy be produced, it is quite open by the law of nations for the inhabitants to form a government *ex necessitate* for the protection of life and property, and such a government has certain sovereign rights *jus gentium*, which might be very convenient for the United States, but exceedingly inconvenient for you. The temptation to an acknowledgement of such a government by the United States would be very great, and ought not to be lightly risked.

" 'We have formally notified the Colonial Office by cable of the situation of affairs, and stated the helplessness and inaction of the Hudson's Bay authorities. We have thrown the responsibility on the Imperial Government, and they will doubtless urge the Hudson's Bay people by cable to take active and vigorous steps. Meanwhile, your course has been altogether right. By staying at Pembina you will be at an easy distance from the territory, and can, it is hoped, open communication with the insurgent leaders.'

"See that the fool gets it before he does anything really stupid."

The fool did not. On December 1, he crossed the border to the Hudson's Bay Company's fort, and read his proclamation. By its terms, the Hudson's Bay Company's authority was terminated, and he was now Governor of the province. Further, Lieutenant Colonel John Dennis was now the "Conservator of the Peace," empowered to raise an army and take whatever action was necessary to quell the insurrection that was threatening the territory.

It was a cold and grey day, threatening snow. The ground was frozen hard underfoot, and the snow that had already fallen lay blown into hostile drifts. McDougall remembered Ambroise Lépine and his band of armed *métis*. He read his proclamation in the cold, drafty fort, and scurried back to Pembina, to face raucous laughter, jeers, and cries of "Welcome home, Governor!"

And a new flag was flying over Fort Garry—a gold *fleur de lis* on a white background, the symbol of the provisional government of Red River.

19

HENRY Sleight came back to Oak Point for just a couple of days, to spend some time with Anna Lee before returning to Winnipeg and the conflict that was shaking the whole settlement.

Charlotte grabbed him and took him aside as soon as he walked in the house, before he even had a chance to ask for Anna Lee.

"There's something I have to talk to you about, Henry," she said. "Anna Lee will still be there—you can see her later."

"All right, Mrs. Graham. What is it?"

"Have you seen James?"

"James? No, I haven't seen him. Has something happened to him?"

"I don't know. He's just gone. He disappeared from the house three days ago."

"I'm sure there's an explanation."

"I'm sure there is, too. I think he's gone to join up with

Dr. Schultz. That's why I was wondering if you'd seen him."

"No, I haven't, but if he only left here three days ago, I would have missed him anyway. If he is with Dr. Schultz, then I'll see him soon enough, when I get back to Winnipeg."

Anna Lee had come down the stairs, and when she heard Henry's voice she approached the parlor, but slowed up as she got there, and stood just outside the door to listen for a moment. The first thing that she heard was Henry talking about going back to Winnipeg, and she shook her head angrily. She was about to burst into the room, but something in her mother's tone of voice made her want to hold back and not interrupt, not just yet.

"Tell him to come home," Charlotte said.

"I'll tell him when I see him. I don't know if he'll listen to me, though."

Charlotte began to cry, surprising Henry, who had never thought of her as having an emotional side.

But if Henry was surprised, Anna Lee was profoundly astonished. The idea that her mother would let down her guard, would be anything but calculating and in control under any circumstance, was almost more than she could believe.

For a brief instant, she wanted to go to her and put her arms around her. But that feeling was followed by one of revulsion. She did not want to have anything to do with her mother's human side. It was too late.

But she could not turn away from it, either. She stayed in the shadows, and listened to the rest of the conversation.

"He's still just a baby. He should be home with his mother."

"He's sixteen years old, Mrs. Graham. That's pretty young, but not so young that he can't take care of himself on his own."

"But there's going to be trouble . . . terrible trouble. It's not safe."

"I don't think there'll be any trouble, Mrs. Graham. There hasn't been any fighting, and I'm sure there won't be. This will all be straightened out peacefully in good time."

Charlotte was not consoled. She kept on weeping, and the more she cried, the more she seemed like an infant herself.

Flustered, Sleight went to put his arm around her to try and comfort her, but he felt too awkward in that position. He had second thoughts, and his arms stopped halfway up, and stayed in that position for a moment, his hands fluttering awkwardly like the featherless wings of a baby bird. Charlotte, her head buried deep in her own sobs, did not appear to notice.

"I'll certainly talk to him when I see him, Mrs. Graham. I'll see to it that he gets home safely. Well, I should go and find Anna Lee. It's nice to see you, Mrs. Graham. And I'll certainly give James a good talking-to for you. I'll send him right home, don't worry about that."

He prattled on as he backed out of the room. Anna Lee retreated into the kitchen so as not to be caught eavesdropping, and then came from there back out into the hall to greet Henry.

But she gave herself away, if Henry had been of a mood to notice such things, with the first words out of her mouth:

"What's this I hear about your going back to Winnipeg? Henry, you can't do that! Not now—I need you here with me."

"I'll be back soon enough, dearest. This business will be over soon."

"But what about us? We're supposed to be getting married."

"We set the wedding date for next June, remember? I'll certainly be back before then."

"There's no reason why we can't move it up. Why should we have to wait? Let's get married right away—this week—and move away from here. We can move to Ontario. I don't want to stay here any more. And I don't want you to go away again."

"We can't do it, dearest. We can't move to Ontario on no income, and I won't know what I'm worth financially until this business is settled," Henry told her. "I don't know what's going to happen to the property rights in Red River, and everything I have is tied up in this land speculation."

"I don't care. I'd be willing to start out with nothing."

"Well, I care. And so do you. You aren't dreaming about moving to Ontario because of your fondness for roughing it. And living in a sod shanty on the frontier is nothing compared to being poor and living in the city. I came out here to get rich, and especially now that I will have a wife and family to support, I'm committed to staying here until that happens, and to doing whatever I can to make sure that it does happen."

He was right, and Anna Lee knew it. She did want to live comfortably. That was a major part of her dream of moving to Ontario.

She had made the decision to put Louis Riel out of her life, and she stuck to it tenaciously. Not being with Louis was the most important thing to her now, as important as being with Louis had once been. That was part of Ontario, too—not being in a place where Riel's name was on everybody's lips, and no one could escape being aware of his every movement.

And not being with Louis also meant that she no longer wanted for herself the life she had been willing to embrace when she was with Louis—poverty, struggle, idealistic self-sacrifice. It was not for her. She did want the better things in life.

So she cried, in her turn, and vented her anger on Henry Sleight, but then she let him go. She stayed on in Oak Point, as far as she could be from Winnipeg and Fort Garry. She stayed in her room as much as she could, away from her family, and away from the constant conversation that went on in the store on the subject of Louis Riel and his *métis* government.

Sleight got back to Winnipeg December 6, and went straight to the home of Dr. John Schultz.

It no longer looked like a home. Schultz had sent his wife and children away, and moved in a battalion of armed men, who were bivouacked around every available square inch of space. The doors and windows had been fortified, and the kitchen had become a military headquarters, with maps and plans spread out over all the tables and counter space.

Schultz sat at the table in the center of the room, looking like a commanding general. Behind him was a guard of three men; and one of them, hard-eyed and determined, was young James Graham.

Schultz was putting the finishing touches on a dispatch. He threw down his pen, blotted the ink, and folded the paper over. He handed it to one of the grim-faced men behind him.

"Take this to Dennis," Schultz said. "And for God's sake, be careful!"

"Yes, sir!" The aide-de-camp—that seemed to be the only way to describe him—snapped off the answer. He spun on his heel and walked swiftly to the door, passing Sleight without acknowledging him.

"For God's sake, John, what's going on here?" Sleight asked, pulling up a chair across the table from Schultz, and leaning forward on his forearm to look over Schultz's diagram.

"Yes, sit down, Henry," Schultz said. "We don't have martial law here yet—we can still be informal. Damn near to it, though. What's going on? It's war, that's what. We've got everything we need to take the offensive now, Henry. We've got the authority, we've got the law on our side. McDougall's taken over, and he's appointed Dennis as military commander of the province. We can run those bastards out of here, and run them all the way to the Rockies—those of them that live to get that far."

"Do you think it's going to be that easy, John? Having legal authority is one thing, but being able to implement it can be another. Dennis doesn't have very many men. And I don't mean to be unkind, but neither do you, for that matter."

"We have a good core of troops, and they're white men. They're not going to turn tail and run like a bunch of filthy half-breeds. And that's not all. Dennis has those Enfield rifles from McDougall, and we've enlisted a company of Swampy Indians to fight on our side."

"You've given rapid-firing rifles to the Swampy Indians?" Sleight asked incredulously. The Swampy tribe were widely distrusted in the territory by *métis* and other Indian tribes alike, a renegade bunch whose primary means of making a living was stealing cattle.

"Yes, that should give us the men we need for a successful night attack on Fort Garry."

"Are you sure that's wise? The Indians—"

"Aren't nearly as much of a threat to us as those damned half-breeds are. We can take care of the Indians later."

Sleight tried one more tack. "John, I don't think it would be so impossible to come to terms with Riel and his men. I mean, they've said openly that all they're trying to create is a provisional government, and that if McDougall agrees to their list of rights, they'll escort him into Fort Garry themselves, and turn the government over to him immediately."

Schultz's face grew iron-hard. "*List of rights*! Good God, man, we're talking about a bunch of rebels! Anarchists! And we're talking about our own futures, too, and you'd do well not to forget that. We've got a lot invested in this land, and it's going to be a great country some day. A province of Canada! Not some sort of reservation for half-breeds."

"I know, John. But sometimes you have to compromise. This struggle could drag on and on. We could lose what we already have.

I guarantee you that we will not lose a damned thing. And I don't care how long it takes. The longer it drags on, the more completely we'll crush them in the end, and the more we'll have to divide among the desirable citizens of this territory."

As they were talking, another of Schultz's volunteers came in, stood before the table, and saluted.

"The flag is here, sir."

"Good. Come on outside, Henry."

Sleight followed, along with James Graham and the rest of Schultz's men. When the entire company was assembled outside, Sleight calculated it to be about fifty men.

The flag was unfolded—the maple leaf flag of Canada. The entire garrison stood at attention as the flag of what they were proclaiming as their country was raised on a flagpole above Dr. John Schultz's house, and a piper played "Rule, Britannia."

Sleight stood at attention, too, but he looked at Schultz closely, trying to figure out if the man had gone mad. No, he decided. Not at all. This was the same John Schultz he had always known—a man who knew what he wanted, and was pressing his advantage in every way he could to make sure that he got it.

The playing of "Rule, Britannia" concluded. The maple leaf flag unfurled itself from the top of the flagpole, and flapped in the chill winter wind. The company stood at ease.

"Welcome to Fort Schultz, Henry," the doctor said.

Henry Sleight stayed at Fort Schultz that night, billeted with the rest of the "troops." He talked for a while to James Graham—long enough to convince himself that there was nothing he could say to make the boy go back home to his mother. James Graham had found his calling in life, it seemed—as a soldier in Dr. John Schultz's army, dedicated to wiping out the *métis* and driving them, every last one of them, out of the Red River settlement, which belonged by right to decent Christian—that was to say, Protestant—white men and their families.

Talking to James was too depressing for Henry, and he gave it up. He was too afraid that he himself had sounded just like that, and not so long ago.

So he found a pallet on the floor, lay down with his eyes open, and thought about what he was doing.

He knew that although he had made some inroads on his original reputation in Red River, he was still thought of in most people's minds as the stuffed shirt whom old Mrs. Richards had horsewhipped in the general store, or as the arrogant bigot who had insulted *Métis* womanhood in his letter to the Toronto *Globe*.

Or as Dr. John Schultz's lackey. Or as the future son-in-law of Schultz's partner Charlotte Graham, as the man who was going to marry the woman that Louis Riel was well rid of.

Well, it was all true, in a way. He still wore tweeds, still looked like an outsider, still spoke in a fancy accent and occasionally used rhetorical flourishes that sounded pompous to the natives. He was still tied economically to the Canadian party and to Schultz. He knew that his own prosperity depended on Schultz's land deals holding up, and on Schultz's group having the primary influence in the new government.

But he would have preferred to compromise more, if the choice had been left to him. He no longer was so sure that the *métis* had to be driven out of Red River in order to achieve success for their side. He was quite sure that there was no moral right to that position.

And he was fascinated by Louis Riel. He was most impressed by the man's intelligence, leadership, and conviction.

Especially, though, he was fascinated by the fact that the woman he was going to marry had loved Louis Riel passionately.

He would have liked to have gotten to know Riel better. If such a thing were at all possible, he would have liked to volunteer himself as a mediator between the two sides. But it did not appear that there was going to be any mediation.

Sleight's lot was cast, and he knew it. He closed his eyes, and went to sleep in Fort Schultz.

When he awoke the next morning, Fort Schultz was surrounded. Two cannon from Fort Garry were aimed directly at the front door.

There was no possibility of a fight. Schultz, Sleight, James Graham, and forty-five others were arrested and brought into Fort Garry, prisoners of Louis Riel's provisional government of the Northwest Territory.

20

WHILE they were imprisoned in Fort Garry, Sleight and Schultz heard the news. First, Dennis had been recalled by the Canadian government, to face a severe reprimand for his irresponsible and reckless acts of "Conservator of the Peace" in Red River. Then, a week before Christmas, McDougall packed up and left Pembina. He headed back for Ottawa, his dreams of a power base in the Northwest now as empty and abandoned as the fort just north of the border where he had proclaimed himself governor of the Northwest.

Louis Riel's provisional government now seemed to be in complete control.

Schultz only snorted at the idea. "He'll go too far. His kind always do. The man's a fanatic. He'll lose everything."

They spent Christmas in prison. The *métis* were not harsh jailers. They made Christmas dinner for their prisoners, and allowed wives and families to come in and visit, to bring gifts or food and drink.

Sleight knew that he would not get a visit from Anna Lee. She was not about to set foot in Fort Garry while it was under Louis Riel's command, and Sleight did not expect any different. He had written to her, though, to let her know he was all right.

He also wrote to Charlotte, to assure her that James was alive and in good health. James was not one to bother himself with writing—indeed, it was a skill that he had wasted very little time in learning.

Riel himself did not visit the prison compound. Sleight was disappointed.

A dozen prisoners promised to support the provisional government, and were released on their word. A few more disappeared one night, and another couple the week after. They had escaped, and no one seemed to care a great deal, as long as the ringleaders were still securely under lock and key.

James Graham was one of the latter group of escapees, and Sleight was glad of it. He hoped that the boy would go home to his mother.

Then one night a fellow prisoner in Sleight's compound discovered that a door had not been locked properly, and he called Sleight over.

"Look at this," he whispered. "It didn't quite catch right. We can get it open."

"Are you sure?" Sleight asked.

"I know about locks. If you put your weight against the door, give it some pressure, and I fool around with the catch, I can pop it. We'll have to watch for the guard, though. I can't do it quietly."

"He only comes around once every couple of hours. Let's wait until he comes by again, and then we'll be sure of it."

The guard came and went. Sleight watched him out of sight, then put his shoulder to the door, and pushed as the other man worked the lock. The door sprang open with a thud, but no one came to investigate. They were free.

"Should we get Schultz?"

"Let's just go," Sleight said. "He can take care of himself."

"Nah. We'd better get him."

"I suppose we'd better."

Ten of them, ultimately, left the prison yard and climbed over the wall of the fort. It was night, and the temperature was twenty-five degrees below zero. They were in Winnipeg, a town that had a few sympathizers to their cause, but not many. If they wanted to be safe, they had to get out of town before their captors realized they were missing, and make for one of the nearby Scottish farms owned by a sympathizer.

"Let's just find a livery stable and steal some horses."

"No, we need supplies, too," Schultz said. "Food and guns."

"What do you want to do? Rob a store? We can't take a chance like that."

"That's not necessary. A house will do fine. We'll surprise whoever's there and take what we need. We can tie them up or take them hostage if we need them."

Sleight was dubious. Schultz overrode his objections.

"There are ten of us, man! Nobody's going to overpower us, and nobody's going to get away to sound an alarm, either. Now, come on."

They picked a small house with a single oil lamp lit in the window. They surrounded it, and Schultz burst in through the front door, with Sleight and two others behind him.

A tired woman of about forty sat in front of the fireplace. On the floor at her feet was a boy, playing with a top. He looked to be too old for that sort of game, but it was hard to tell how old he was. Somewhere in his teens—his face was too bland and sweet to be any guide to how much life he had lived. He shrank closer to his mother when the four haggard, menacing figures strode in, while she dropped the book she was reading and put her hand on his shoulder.

"Don't shout or try anything and you won't get hurt," Schultz commanded. "Is there anybody else in this house?"

"Only the baby upstairs," the woman said. "Who are you?"

"Is she telling the truth?" Schultz demanded of the boy.

Instead of replying, he turned and buried his cheek against his mother's dress.

"Answer when you're spoken to," Schultz said sharply. "What's the matter with him?"

"He's slow, that's all. Brain never growed up proper. He get's scared easy. Don't talk much. But he's a good boy."

Schultz laughed gutturally. "Looks like a typical half-breed to me," he said, jerking his head back over his shoulder.

Sleight felt sick.

"Do you have any guns in the house?" Schultz demanded.

The woman pointed to a double barreled shotgun on the wall. Striding over, Schultz yanked it down off the hooks that held it, pulling one of them loose as he did so.

"Loaded?"

Even as she was nodding her head up and down, Schultz was cracking open the gun to verify for himself that there was a shell in each chamber.

"All right. We'll need food, too. Tell him to get it. Bring us whatever you've got in the house. We'll need it all."

By this time, the others had all satisfied themselves that no one was going to slip out the back or sides of the house, and they had all come in, one at a time. The boy's eyes had widened with each new intruder, but he still pressed against his mother's knee, and did not move.

"It's all right, Claude," the woman said. "Do as the gentleman says. Go and get him food."

Still the boy did not move, and the mother gently moved her knee back, and disengaged his hands from her knee.

"Go *on*, Claude," she said, still gently. "Do as mama says."

The boy got up then, and dawdled across the room, dragging one foot and making circular patterns with it on the floor. He seemed lost in something that was not quite thought, in a world of his own.

"*Move it, boy*!" Schultz snarled at him.

The harsh sounds hit the retarded boy like a whip. He cringed, twisted his body away, and stopped in the middle of the room.

"Idiot! Do as you're told!"

The boy let out a cry of pain. Suddenly, he turned and rushed at Schultz, his big, awkward body picking up momentum and his arms flailing.

"*What . . .?*" Schultz reacted swiftly. He brought the gun butt up and hit the boy in the head.

The boy staggered a step backwards. Blood flowed down in his face, but he was still standing. He cried out again in fury, and lunged again. Schultz sidestepped, and caught him hard at the base of the skull as he passed by.

This time the boy went down, but the men by the door, as whose feet he had fallen, could see that his eyes were still open, and that they had taken on an expression of frightening clarity, not confusion. Sleight reached down to give the boy a hand, but he regained his feet by himself. He swung his forearm at Sleight like a club, knocking him down. Then, coughing and shrieking like a wounded elk he ran for the door.

The men near the door were too stunned to move.

Schultz got there before any of them. He raised the shotgun to his shoulder, and fired.

The first shot hit the boy in the side, and spun him around with such force that the second hit him right in the face. Blood spattered everywhere, sliding across the frozen surface of the snow, steaming and then starting to freeze itself.

"Let's get out of here," Schultz grunted.

They ran out into the night, each in different directions, as faces appeared in doorways, lanterns sprang up in windows, and somewhere near by, an alarm bell began to ring.

They caught Sleight before he had gone half a mile. Everywhere there were angry, vigilant *métis* with guns, clubs, pitchforks. Sleight was beaten before they brought him back to the fort, but he hardly felt it. He wished he had felt it more.

He was lined up with the other captured escapees, nine of them in all. The only one missing, the only one who had made a clean getaway, was Dr. John Schultz. Sleight was later to hear that he was safely in Toronto, living the life of a social lion and stirring up hatred and racial antagonism against the provisional government.

21

SLEIGHT was not sure how long it had been since he had last been conscious. Three or four days, he guessed, by the feel of his beard.

He remembered the blood before he remembered anything else. Then the rest of it came back to him: the boy's face, exploding in the snow. Running. Being caught, beaten. Yes, he had been beaten. He could feel it now: he ached all over.

Yes, and he felt feverish. He remembered being brought back to prison, now. He must have passed out in his cell.

He rubbed his beard again. Three, maybe four days.

He tried to open his mouth, but found it painful and difficult. He tried to speak, and that was harder still. His voice was only a croak.

"Water . . . can I have . . . some . . . water, please?"

A guard looked in through the window of his cell.

"Hey . . . he's awake."

* * *

The fever might still have been affecting his perception, or the darkness of the cell, suddenly brightened by the oil lamp the newcomer brought with him, may have made a difference. All Sleight knew for sure was that there seemed to be something extraordinary, something almost more than mortal, about the man who stood in front of him.

He wondered, at that moment, whether this might have been the reason why he had stayed on in Winnipeg, stayed involved in the conflict, even gotten himself arrested: the desire, the need, to come face to face once more with Louis Riel.

He had been struck by the firmness of Riel's presence during the confrontation at Andre Nault's field. But the man seemed to have grown along with his reputation, and along with the faith and power entrusted to him.

He appeared to have grown even in physical stature. He loomed over Sleight, the oil lamp's flickering light spreading his shadow out until it embraced the whole cell. His face was in shadow, but his eyes burned. And when he spoke, his voice reverberated off the damp, deadened, cold cell walls.

"Where is Schultz?" he asked.

Sleight only blinked.

"Where is Dr. John Schultz?"

"He was with us."

"He was not caught with you."

"That's right . . . I remember now . . . didn't see him when they brought us back in." Sleight sat up straighter, struggled to clear his head, and steady his voice. Then he said, as firmly as he could, "Mr. Riel, I give you my word that I would not try to shield Dr. John Schultz if I knew where he was."

He could feel Riel's burning eyes probing him, and he knew that Riel must know he was telling the truth. He could not have lied under that scrutiny.

Riel left without saying another word.

* * *

It took Sleight a week to recover. After his audience with Riel, he slept for another twenty-four hours, and awoke in a sweat and chills. They gave him strong tea and herbs, and the fever broke. The day after that, he was allowed to walk outside in the pale winter sunshine for a few minutes, then given more tea, more of the herbal preparation.

Finally, he was strong again. They gave him a razor and hot water, and permitted him to clean himself up. And he was given another audience with Riel.

This time he was ushered into Riel's austere office, and given a chair across from where the *métis* leader was sitting.

"We talked to the dead boy's mother," Riel said. "It seems clear that the man who actually pulled the trigger was Schultz."

"That is so."

"We are also satisfied that no one but Schultz had any idea of doing harm to the family."

"Yes, that's true, too. None of the rest of us even wanted to go into the house. I'm not trying to absolve myself of responsibility. It's just that I was shocked and revolted by what happened I want to make it clear, as I told you before, that in no way can I condone what Schultz did, and I would not protect him."

"I'm glad to hear you say you are not trying to absolve yourself of responsibility," Riel said.

"No, of course not," Sleight answered. "I wouldn't do that."

"Because you realize that a retarded boy was murdered in cold blood, during the commission of a felony against the only government in the Northwest, and the people of Red River are outraged. They are clamoring for some sort of reprisal."

"I see."

"Yes. And you, of all the escapees, are most closely identified as an associate of Dr. John Schultz. And of course, there is widespread bitterness against your name in Red River, on its own merits."

"Of course. And I can understand what you're saying. At the same time, I cannot believe that you are saying it. What you propose—what you are hinting at—would have every semblance of justice in some people's eyes. Would it be justice in yours?"

"That, Mr. Sleight, may not be the question."

Sleight held his breath for a moment.

"I think that as far as I'm concerned, it may be the only question."

"Indeed. You're a brave man, Mr. Sleight, to be concerned about the moral fiber of your adversary rather than your own life."

"No, I'm scared enough. It's just that I don't see that it's likely to make much difference. So I may as well prepare to die at least knowing something more about the man who's willing to see the deed done. I'd like to know whether I'm being sacrificed to a principle or to expediency."

"Hmm . . . you may have a point, Mr. Sleight. Then again . . . it's true that the provisional government wants to put you on public trial for murder. So far, I've been able to forestall it."

As winter turned into spring, the provisional government was maintaining order in Red River. Ottawa had sent representatives to negotiate with them, and to work out an agreement for annexation on terms that would be acceptable to the Red River community. They were willing to be very agreeable at this point, especially since the United States was waiting in the wings, with annexationist ideas of its own.

And over those weeks, Riel and Sleight met on a number of occasions. They continued fencing with each other, and as they did so, they were gradually building up a kind of grudging, careful admiration and trust for each other.

For Sleight, it was fascinating. He had never known anyone like Riel. He envied the other man his strength, his commitment, even his fanaticism. Sleight had never had an ideal to believe in, the way that Riel did. His only model for a dedicated, committed man was Dr. John Schultz, and Schultz was nothing like Riel. His commitment was to profit and power, and nothing else.

The relationship between Sleight and Riel teetered back and forth. Sleight could never forget that the ultimate stake in this game was his life, and that Riel could . . . might be able to influence that decision, if he only would.

Sometimes Sleight's anger, bitterness and frustration would get the better of him, and he would simply lash out in fury at Riel, so bitterly that he was sure his captor would leave and never come back.

But Riel never left in the middle of one of Sleight's tirades. His comings and goings, which were always abrupt, seemed to be geared to some inner voice rather than anything that Sleight said.

And he always came back.

Other times, Sleight might be in a philosophical mood, during which he would reminisce about his past, and exchange childhood memories with Riel.

But he preferred it when Riel talked. When Riel was feeling open, he would open up candidly about his personal dreams, about the importance of the *métis* cause for him, about his education as a seminarian and the battle of faith that he was still fighting.

He came down to Sleight's cell one afternoon, late, as the light came in on a sharp slant through Sleight's one window, and made a patch on the wall opposite. Everything else was in shadow.

Riel sat in the shadow. His face bore the same epic solemnity it always had, and yet Sleight thought that there was more going on behind it this time.

"Sleight, you have the qualities of a leader. I'd like to ask you to join my government. I need a man like you as a liaison to the English community. But I can't forestall the people's demands for justice any longer. There's too much pressure. You will go on trial for murder tomorrow."

"Well, old man, I must say that's quite a . . ." Sleight started out to make a jaunty, casual retort, but he could not sustain it, and the reality of the situation silenced him.

When he spoke again, his voice quivered with fear and anger.

"That's a hell of a thing to do to anyone, Riel! How can you even say both of those things in the same breath? To a man you claim to respect . . . and I even thought we'd come to be friends over the last weeks! How can you . . . are you crazy, man?"

"Don't blaspheme in front of me," Riel began, but then his face, too, clouded over and contorted with pain. "Sometimes I think it will tear me apart," he said in a low, still voice.

"What?"

Riel shook his head. He started to say something more, but no words came out. His face was drawn into an ill-fitting mask. His skin suddenly looked dry and parched, stretched across his skull as though it had shrunk to a size too small for the bone structure underneath, and his eyes protruded.

Sleight began to feel his body growing damp with sweat all over. His skin itched from inside, and his heart was beating faster and heavier than it should have. He could scarcely talk, and more than Riel could, but his anger prodded him on.

"Perhaps you wouldn't be so anxious to see me on the gallows if I weren't engaged to be married to Anna Lee Graham."

Riel stiffened as if he had been shot, but Sleight could not tell if he had really hit a mark, or if it was just Anna Lee's name that had affected Riel. In any event, Riel shook his head.

"I am not anxious to see you hanged."

"Call it what you like. You could intervene and stop this whole thing, but you won't."

"That is not personal, Mr. Sleight. I could use my influence with the *métis* people in a lot of ways I choose not to—many of which would directly relate to my personal gain. But I will in no way oppose my will to the will of my people."

"I don't want to die!"

"Neither did that boy."

The square of light had risen up the wall as they talked—like a soul ascending to heaven, or a prisoner to the gallows. It was blurred as Riel left the cell, and a jailer locked the door behind him. It had lost its square symmetry to the silhouette of the trees that the sun was sinking behind. Then it was gone, and the room was just grey, and getting darker fast.

22

"I heard from James today, dear," Charlotte said. He's safe. He's been hiding up at our old cabin by Lake Winnipeg, where we had the store when you were little. Now he's coming—"

"Mama, I've been thinking. I think I'm going to—"

"Did you hear me, Anna Lee? I said your brother's safe. He's alive! And he's coming home."

"Yes, I heard, mother. I'm glad he's alive. I just have other things on my mind right now, that's all I want to—"

"The message says that he thinks it's safe to travel now, and—"

"Mama, I don't care! Listen to me. I'm trying to tell you something."

"Don't care? How can you not care? I'm talking about your brother!"

"I can't help it. You know that James and I never got along. I'm sorry but it just means more to you than it does to me."

"Well, I just don't understand how you can say such a thing."

If you listened to me, if you knew me at all, you'd understand, Anna Lee thought.

But she did not try to interrupt any more, as her mother went on talking about James, and what a blessing it was that he was safe, and how wonderful it would be to see him home again.

If her mother did not want to know what she was planning, there was no need to tell her. She went upstairs after breakfast, and began to pack a carpetbag.

She paused by her closet, and thought about it. Her hand reached out for her prettiest dress, then pulled back. No, nothing too expensive, nothing too stylish, nothing that looked as though it could only have been bought in a fine store in Canada.

She chose a simple, homespun dress instead, folded it neatly, and put it into the carpetbag. Packing did not take her long. The sun was still new to the day, and as yet in a standoff with the dawn's chill, when she made ready to leave. She put a light shawl over her shoulders; and, knowing she would not need it in another hour, when the sun rose higher in the sky, she left room for it in the top of her carpetbag.

Charlotte stopped her at the door.

"Where do you think you're going?"

"To Fort Garry."

"Fort Garry? What are you talking about? You can't just go waltzing off to Fort Garry without asking me about it!"

"I can and I'm going to, Mama. I wouldn't have gone without *telling* you about it, but I couldn't talk to you this morning. You had something more important on your mind."

"Anna Lee, that's not true. I don't think that James is

more important than you. I was just worried about him, that's all. I was just glad to hear from him."

"Whatever you say, Mama. Now, if you'll excuse me, I have a train to catch."

Charlotte started to protest again, but suddenly she seemed to change her mind. She looked at Anna Lee and saw a young woman who was no longer hers to order about, and she knew it. Worse than that, she saw a young woman who was almost a complete stranger to her, who did not know her and, Charlotte was very much afraid, did not even like her.

"You're going to try to help Henry, then?"

"That's right."

"You're going to talk to . . . that man?"

"That's right, Mama. Now I really have to go. I'll write you."

"Would you come and sit with me before you go? Would you talk to me for a few minutes?"

"I tried to do that earlier this morning."

"I know. I'm sorry. I should have listened to you. Can we try again now?"

"It's no use—" but there was something in Charlotte's tone that got to Anna Lee, and she relented. "All right," she said. "Let's sit down and talk, then. But only for a few minutes. I have to go."

They took chairs across from each other in the parlor, and Anna Lee waited for her mother to begin. Charlotte seemed smaller than Anna Lee knew her to be, and ill at ease.

Now that she was finally ready to talk to her daughter, Charlotte did not know where to begin. She looked around the parlor, as if it might offer some clue. She looked at the etchings on the wall. There was a pastoral scene from England; a depiction of the Intendant's Palace at Quebec, Drawn on the Spot by Richard Short and engraved by

William Elliot, showing a simple but sumptuous palace and a somewhat ruder courtyard, with cobblestones, horse-drawn carts and prancing dogs; a sentimental engraving of a mother and a fat child, its neck craned at an impossible angle. She looked at the spinet piano from England, the sideboard from France, the carpet on the floor brought back from the Orient by clipper ship, and purchased from one of the finest merchants in Toronto.

"We haven't done badly, have we?" she said to Anna Lee, sounding more defensive than proud. "We've come a long way from that little store by Lake Winnipeg."

"I suppose so."

"You think . . . you think that I've favored James over you?"

She waited for a response from Anna Lee; and when she got none, she went on again as though she were picking up in midsentence, as though she had never expected Anna Lee to say anything at all.

"Well, I suppose I can understand that. It's my fault. I always thought that you knew . . . thought that it would be harder for James, and that I had to . . . but no, I don't suppose . . ."

Her voice kept trailing off, and then starting up again. Each time, she seemed to think that she could complete the thought that she started out with, and each time, she clamped a lid down on it, and would not let it out.

"I've never told you very much about my younger days, have I?"

"No, you haven't."

"Well, they were . . ." No, she was not going to finish that one, either.

There was nothing she could say to her daughter. They were completely cut off from each other.

"They were very hard."

"Yes, I'm sure they were, Mama. I really do have to go now."

"Anna Lee, don't let that Riel person hurt you! Don't let him take advantage of you! Take care of yourself, please . . ."

The words came tumbling out, as though they could somehow take the place of all the words not said, this morning or over the years, but Anna Lee was not even listening to them.

"Yes, Mama. I'll take care, Mama. Please don't worry, Mama."

And she was gone.

She took the American route, by train and carriage, to Pembina. When she prepared to leave Pembina after the formalities of the customs house, and the *métis* cart driver carried out the single bag which she could just as easily have handled herself, and placed it in the back of the cart, she felt a stab of the guilt of the priveleged.

The cart driver was old; it was hard to tell how old. His face was lined with wrinkles, but it was still defined by an aristocratic aquiline nose, a sharp jaw, and high cheekbones that the wrinkled skin still swept down over without sagging. He was the color of his buckskin jacket, a deep, even-toned *bois-brulé*.

Anna Lee tried to engage him in conversation as they took the dusty trail up to Winnipeg, adjusting her voice to a pitch and volume that could be heard over the squeal of the Red River cart.

"I've been to Winnipeg before, you know. I used to live there."

The driver nodded noncommittally. He did not seem to know who she was, and she was glad of it. He clucked to his team of elderly but sturdy cart horses, and they plodded on.

"Has it changed much, since the provisional government took command?"

"Not much."

"That's good. I mean, I'm glad there aren't any hardships, any deprivations or shortages without the Hudson's Bay Company to provide assistance."

"Things are always hard."

"What do you think of M. Riel?"

"Good man. Is a true *métis*."

"And have you heard anything about the Englishman who was put on trial?"

"I hear about trial."

"Do you think it's right? Do you think it's fair, that they . . . what they're planning to do to him?"

The *métis* cart driver's jaw rolled open, and a brown overflow of tobacco juice rolled out onto his chin. He slurped it back into his mouth, spat, and rolled his lower jaw down again, as the sharp corners of his mouth curved up through the wrinkles to touch the fine, high line of his cheekbones.

"Ah, hah, hah," he laughed. "Hah, hah, hah, hah, hah."

23

ANNOUNCING herself was a difficulty she had not even considered, but it was suddenly one of the hardest parts of her whole mission. She had pictured herself walking into a room where Louis was standing, confronting him face to face. She had not imagined having to say her name to a stone-faced stranger, who would then insist that she wait while he conveyed her presence to the President, who could then decide whether or not he wanted to see her.

"Can't you just let me in?" she said. "M. Riel know who I am. It's very important that I see him."

"Just give me your name, mademoiselle," the stony-faced one replied. "The President is a busy man."

She understood. She just could not bring herself to do it. "Can't you just . . ."

"I'm sorry, mademoiselle." Clearly, he did not have much patience for this. "It is impossible."

"Anna Lee Graham," she said under her breath, and rapidly.

"Excuse me?"

"*Annaleegraham.*"

He raised his eyebrows. As she had feared, the name was not unfamiliar to him. She was part of the folklore of a great man; and she was sure enough that she was not cast as the heroine.

"If you will wait here, Mademoiselle Graham—"

In her mind, she ran away.

But she was still standing in the same spot when the stony-faced *métis* came back.

He did not speak to her. He just walked up, stopped in front of her, squared his heels, and then turned and walked back in the direction he had come from.

Anna Lee assumed that meant that she was to follow him, and so she did. He led her through the rough wooden building that had been designed as both the military headquarters and the chief trading post of the old fort, and showed its importance by its size rather than by the sophistication of its architecture. The floors were well-worn, unfinished wood, the beams were rough-hewn, and the walls with their sod chinks looked as though they had never been finished. But there was a long, wide hallway that led to the president's office, and a number of *métis* seemed to be lounging around in it. They all looked up as Anna Lee passed by, following a couple of paces behind her guide, and feeling like . . .

Like a condemned man walking to the gallows. Anna Lee could not keep the thought from her mind, though it chilled her even more to think it; but at the same time it gave her courage. She had a reason to be there, a reason that was much greater than her feelings of trepidation at having to face Louis Riel once again.

The young *métis* opened the door at the end of the corridor for her, and stepped aside so that she could enter.

He did not follow her in, but closed the door behind her with a sharp click.

Riel was standing near the window, with his back to her.

It was such a familiar sight; as familiar to her, Anna Lee realized, as his face. She had seen it turned to her so often, during those terrible days when she answered his summonses to meet him, and never knew whether he would greet her passionately or reject her coldly.

Her heart pounded, and she tried to control it by squeezing her forearms tightly with her hands, and pressing her arms hard against her ribcage.

And she knew that if she went to touch him, his shoulders would be like rocks, the muscles stiff and unyielding to her touch.

Would this be like those days all over again, and would he refuse to turn around and acknowledge her presence at all? No; this time he turned to face her just a few moments after he heard the click of the doorlatch behind her.

"Hello, Louis," she said.

He did not respond to her right away. He only stood and looked at her with an expression so formidable that she wondered whether she had made a mistake in addressing him the way she had always been used to. Perhaps now he would answer to nothing except *"M. le President."*

She did not know if she could bring herself to call him that. But if that was what it would take to save Henry's life . . .

She cleared her throat to begin again, but he spoke before she could.

"Hello, Anna Lee. It's good to see you again."

"I suppose you can guess why I'm here."

"Maybe you'd better tell me."

"It's . . . it's . . . you're looking well, Louis."

"Thank you."

"And you've made such a name for yourself."

"I'm not trying to make a name for myself."

Anna Lee knew that it was true. And that she had made a serious error. Louis was angry now, and she did not know if the could win back his favor.

"Of course not—I didn't mean that you were . . . I just meant . . . I hear about you so much, these days . . . of course, that's always very thrilling for me, to hear your name, and people saying such . . ."

She trailed off in embarrassment—was she flattering him too much? Would he think she was being too forward? She had promised herself, before she came, that she would conduct herself with dignity and not try to make love to him to get what she wanted.

But she realized that he was not even listening to her. He could not hear her over the roar of his own thoughts in his ears.

"I have a mission," he said. "I was chosen to fulfill it, and I am its servant. The servant of my mission. The servant of my people. I started out to serve God, you remember . . . and I could have been content serving Him quietly and anonymously, through study and prayer. But I was chosen instead to serve Him by being a leader of the *métis* people. It makes no difference to me. I was chosen for it, and I accepted the calling."

Anna Lee could follow the words, but the emotional force behind them came from a place she did not understand; nor had she ever been to that place inside herself. The outburst seemed to have cleansed away his anger, though. When he finished, he was looking at her as a stranger, but not as an enemy.

"Why did you come here?" he asked.

"I want to ask you to free Henry Sleight."

He accepted the answer with equanimity; he seemed mildly surprised, but not particularly disturbed by it.

Anna Lee had expected just the reverse. She thought that he would know instantly why she had come, and not be in the least surprised. On the other hand, she thought that he would be profoundly disturbed at being confronted by her, after so long a separation, with a plea for the man who had replaced him in her life.

"Henry Sleight . . ." he said. "Henry Sleight . . . yes, of course. He is a particular friend of yours, isn't he?"

"You know he is." Anna Lee was starting to get angry, but she controlled herself. "Yes, he is, Louis. He means a great deal to me, or I wouldn't have come. I know this meeting has to be difficult for both of us. But Henry and I are engaged to be married. I was sure that you must have heard."

"I had heard."

"And he's a good man. You know he is. He doesn't deserve to be executed."

"A boy is dead. A fourteen-year-old, simple-minded boy."

"Henry didn't do it. He couldn't have. He's innocent and you know it."

"That boy was innocent. He had the mind of a baby. And now he's dead, and his death has to be atoned for."

"But not by Henry!"

"I am the leader of these people. They are demanding retribution for a horrible, senseless death, and I have to give it to them."

"What kind of leader would sentence an innocent man to death, just to satisfy the blood-lust of a mob?"

"Every leader who ever lived. Every man who ever had to take responsibility for the common good."

"This isn't the common good!" Anna Lee burst out. "I don't know why you're doing this, but you're behaving like a monster. A horrible, inhuman, fiendish monster!

And you don't have any right to do what you're doing. You're playing God!''

Louis Riel walked over to his desk, and sat down. He reached into a drawer, and took out a large hunting knife that belonged more at the side of a Plains buffalo skinner than a cravatted statesman. He began to balance it on the tips of his fingers. The blade was razor sharp, but he held back just enough from pressing down so that he did not draw blood.

Suddenly, as Anna Lee watched, he drew the knife down the tip of one finger, and left a red line behind it. The red changed quickly from a line to an ever-widening red stain, that flowed down his finger and began to collect in the palm of his hand.

''What did you do that for?'' Anna Lee asked.

''I'm not playing God,'' Riel said. ''I'm a mortal man in God's sight. And I'm not afraid of blood, my own or anyone else's, if it has to be shed in the service of my people's rights. This is a serious business we have undertaken here. Talk is meaningless.''

''You can't impress me with a stupid gesture like that,'' Anna Lee said. ''If you want to impress me, you'll sign your name to a pardon for Henry Sleight. Can you do that?''

''What makes you think I want to impress you?'' demanded Riel.

''I don't care what you want!''

''Don't you?''

Blood was still streaming down Riel's hand. He took a large red bandana out of his pocket, wiped it away, and then wrapped the bandana around his finger. ''Did you really come here to talk about Henry Sleight?''

''Yes!''

''Then why did you stay away for so long? Why, when you could have come at any time to visit the man you're supposed to be marrying? Didn't you want to see him? Didn't you want to bring him freshly baked bread, and kiss his fingertips through the bars? Or could it be that the reason why you never came to Fort Garry before was that you were afraid of what would happen if you saw me?"

"I can't answer that," Anna Lee said, refusing to meet his eyes. "I don't know what I was thinking of, or how much it had to do with you."

"Did you know that Henry Sleight and I became good friends during the period of his incarceration here?" Louis said.

"No, I didn't."

"We talked frequently. He's a very interesting man, even a good man. I would never have suspected it. We talked about a great many things, and we came to understand each other. There was just one subject which we never discussed. Would you care to venture a guess as to what that one subject might have been?"

"No, I can't guess," said Anna Lee, although she was all too afraid that she knew just what it was. "I don't know."

"You're playing the idiot again, just as you always did with me," Louis said. "Oh, yes, I knew. I always knew when you could have given me a straight answer, but you held back from it. And you could tell me now, too. What was the one subject that Henry Sleight and I never, never discussed?"

Anna Lee hung her head.

"Of course, it was you. You were the one subject that neither of us was brave enough to bring up in the other's presence. And yet not a day of our acquaintanceship went by—not one time did I go down to that cell of his, and sit for five or ten minutes, or two or three hours, talking about the state of the Red River settlement, the internal politics of Canada, or differences between the races or the importance of theology and religious beliefs, or even the weather, when the real subject in both of our heads was anything except you."

"You're making fun of me," Anna Lee said.

"You know me better than that. I make fun of nobody. I do not joke; I never learned how, though I have often wished that I could. It is the truth. You were always the real subject of all our discussions, the omnipresent unspoken subject."

"I don't know what to say."

"And the question that was uppermost in both of our minds . . . can you guess that?"

"I don't think so."

"Perhaps not. Maybe you have not yet learned that underneath race, religion, political preferences, values and ideals and dreams of a better mankind, underneath it all a man is a man. The question that I never asked Henry Sleight, I will ask you now. Did you ever make love to him?"

"What?"

"Did you ever know him carnally?"

This was too unbelievable to protest against, too unbelievable to answer with anything except the truth.

"No, I never did. You are the only man who has ever made love to me."

One would have thought, with all the times that Louis Riel claimed to have rehearsed that question, that he would have been able to continue the conversation from there. But he seemed so dumbfounded at actually hearing an answer that he just stood there, and stared at Anna Lee. But he looked pleased, and the almost stupidly pleased expression on his face made Anna Lee angry.

"But he's the man I'm going to marry," she said. "And after that, he will have every right to me as a husband."

"Anna Lee, have you forgotten me?" Louis asked.

"You were the one who forgot me," she said.

"No. I was the one who left you. There's a difference."

"To me, it is a meaningless difference."

"Meaningless, real . . . what does it matter? Let's say that I have forgotten you. I am still slave of my baser emotions enough to want to know whether you ever forgot me."

Anna Lee looked at Louis for a long time before she answered.

"No, Louis," she said at last. "I never forgot you. I can still look at you now standing behind that imposing desk, and see something different. I can still look at those awful depressing black clothes, that priest's outfit that you still try to force your soul into, and see—is this what you wanted to hear, Louis?—and see the body that's standing underneath them. Yes, a man's body, not a priest's body. It is the only man's body I have ever seen, and I know it very well. I know how pale it is, and how much like a baby's it seemed to me sometimes. And I know . . . I know that part of it that I'm not even supposed to know the name of, much less mention, so I will spare your sense of decorum and not call it by name. But I know just what it looks like—when you are excited and want me, and when it's small and shriveled afterwards. And I will never forget any of that."

She was right. He had asked the question; he had even gotten the answer that he must have been hoping for. But he was not prepared to hear it. He cringed before her now, in the way that men cringe who are terrified of women.

"I see all that because I know you so well, Louis. But that's not all I see. I don't know. Maybe I wish it were. In a way it would be wonderful—what every girl wants—to hold onto my first love. Shall I tell you what else I see?"

"Go ahead," he said in a toneless voice.

"I see something in your eyes that came and went before. I didn't want to see it, and when it wasn't there I could pretend that it had never been there, or at least that it would never come back. But it's there now. And even if you wanted me, your wanting would not be able to break through it. You've changed, Louis. Or else you've become more than ever, the self you were always meant to be. You're nothing except your cause now, and your vision of yourself as the leader of a cause. I know that you're a great man, and a great leader. I'm afraid for you, though. I'm afraid that if you don't watch out, you'll start thinking of yourself as a messiah. But I do know that there's no room in your life for a woman. I don't know who there is room in your life for. I'm glad that you were able to become friends with Henry. You're getting near the point where you won't be able to allow a friend into your life at all. Is that why you're killing Henry, then—the real reason? Not because of me at all, but because you let him get too close to you, and you can't dismiss him, the way you can dismiss a mere woman?"

"I am not killing him," Louis said. "He was tried and convicted of murdering a civilian, by a military tribunal. It's all completely legal. We are the government of the Red River settlement. I did not pronounce the sentence of death. It's only my authority to carry it out."

His voice was faltering. His shoulders were no longer squared and unflinching, and his eyes looked unsure as Anna Lee held them in her gaze, until he could no longer look at her, and turned away.

"What do you want me to do?"

"I want you to let him go."

"I can't do that."

She snorted angrily.

Louis went back to the window again, and she saw his

back once more, but it was not the stone wall it had been. He could not block out what she was saying.

"If he escaped," Louis said without turning around, "would you be able to hide him?"

"I could take him to my mother's old place up near Lake Winnipeg," she said. "It's deserted, and safe."

"Get two horses, then," he told her. "Be at the rear gate of the fort tonight as soon as it gets dark."

24

THERE was no making camp for the night. They rode quickly through the town, and more carefully along the northern roads when they got out of town. By the time they got to the back country, where the trails were harder to follow and more treacherous underfoot for the horses, it was dawn, and they could see their way.

Anna Lee knew the way, anyway. She was surprised at how well she remembered it, given that she had not thought about it for years, so she led, and Sleight followed along behind her.

There was little talk while they rode. No time; and besides, they both knew that what they wanted to say to each other was more than could be passed back and forth, over the shoulder, and above the sound of the hoofbeats of two swiftly moving horses.

They reached the abandoned store around the middle of the afternoon. Sleight went to see to the horses, while Anna Lee went inside.

The store was empty. The shelves were bare, and some of them were caved in. Mice had made nests in the corners, birds had constructed them along the broken shelves, and mud dauber wasps had suspended theirs from the rafters. The fireplace had been used from time to time, by travelers. There was still a cast iron kettle hanging from the crossbeam, left there perhaps by Charlotte Graham, perhaps by some traveler who wanted to leave a little bit of himself for those who came after him; and there was a cold, blackened butt of wood below it.

The cabin showed signs of more recent occupancy, and by one who was even messier and more chaotic than the forces of nature. There were a few charred chunks of wood in this fireplace, too, and ashes strewn around the front of it, along with coffee grounds. A plate on the table had dried-out beans stuck to it, and there were more beans scattered across the surface of the table, mingled with mouse droppings.

A tin cup next to the plate held green and white spores of mold growing on top of about a half inch of coffee. Anna Lee took it, and poured it out on the ground outside the front door.

She left the door open, to air the place out. It smelled slightly rancid.

A chair next to the table had been knocked over; Anna Lee set it right.

In a corner was a bare, filthy straw mattress. She took it over to the door and shook it out, raising clouds of dust. Then she laid it back on the floor.

She went and opened the saddlebag she had brought in with her, and unpacked the one luxury item she had brought with her for their getaway. It was a sheet, a clean white linen sheet. She laid it down over the straw mattress, tucking its corners in.

That came first on her list of priorities. She smiled as

she looked down at it. Then she laid a fire and lit it in the fireplace, and went to the cistern outside the cabin door for water, which she put on to boil for coffee. When Henry came in, it was ready, and she put a cup on the table for him, steaming and black, and also one for herself.

He blew on it, and gulped down a couple of swallows to get the taste of the trail out of his mouth.

"I can't believe we're here," he said. "I had started to think of myself as a dead man."

"You certainly don't look like a dead man now," Anna Lee said.

"I can't look as good as you, though," he said. "At best, I look like a mere mortal. You're an angel, if I ever saw one. An angel of mercy, an angel of deliverance. An answer to my prayers, if I ever offered up any. But I suppose I must have offered up one or two, or they wouldn't have sent me an angel, would they?"

"I don't know about that," Anna Lee giggled. "But you look pretty good yourself—especially for a mere mortal."

She was looking at him closely as she said the words, and thinking how true they were. Seeing Louis again was giving her a whole new perspective on Henry, and she began to think about how much he had changed. He was leaner than she remembered him and tougher: of course, prison would do that to a man. But there were other changes that were less predictable. His face was harder, but his eyes were softer. They opened inward more, and she liked what she saw in them.

"You saved my life," Sleight said. "Riel told me about it."

"What did he say?"

"Not very much. He came down to my cell in the afternoon. It was the first time that I had seen him since the trial. And perhaps it's strange, but I was glad to see him. I knew that he'd been staying away because he felt too awkward about seeing me after I'd been sentenced to death by his judge and jury, in his courtroom . . . and well he should have, too. But, I don't know . . . by the time I finally saw him again, yesterday, I'd reconciled myself to the fact that it was going to happen. At least, I felt I had—I suppose it's not the sort of thing one can really reconcile himself to, but one tells stories to make it easier to bear.

"Anyway, I was starting to miss his visits. And if that sounds unlikely to you, just remember that everything takes on a different perspective when one spends a certain amount of time in prison.

"He came in and told me that he'd seen you, and that he was arranging for me to get out. Then he started to leave as abruptly as he came in—moody, the way he is so often. And then he did something he'd never done before. He stopped by the door and said, 'don't talk to your jailers about this.' "

"So that was when you knew it was going to be an escape," Anna Lee said.

"That was when I knew it was going to be an escape. But I didn't know anything else. I waited all afternoon. I was excited, and a little frightened—it's hard not to suspect a trap, when one's life is suddenly and almost capriciously returned to him. And there was something else that preyed on my mind too, all the rest of that afternoon. Riel had said only that he had talked to you, and that he was going to let me go. Nothing about *what* was said—of course, I assumed that you had pleaded for my life, and had somehow won him over.

"But I knew, also, that his moodiness and abruptness—the fact that he could not even bring himself to stay and tell me the details of the plan—had to do with you. Do you know that during all the time I was in prison, and all the time that Riel and I talked to each other—deeply, holding almost nothing in our souls back—we never talked about you?''

''Yes, I know,'' Anna Lee said softly.

''What?''

''Oh. nothing . . . I mean . . . I just . . .'' she caught herself trying to dissemble, and she was amazed at her own foolishness. Surely there was nothing left that could be hidden now. They had all been to the brink together, and it was time for simple, plain speaking.

''Louis told me the same thing, when we talked this afternoon.''

''It's not quite true. Your name did come up—once—the day Riel told me that I was to be put on trial. I was the one who brought it up, but he wouldn't take the bait—because that, of course, was just what it was at the time.

''But he came back, later. He told me how I could get away, and he told me where to meet you. There was time, yet, a couple of hours before I could go. So we sat and talked. And this time, we did talk about you.''

''What did you say?''

Henry took a deep breath, and shook his head. ''Not now,'' he said. ''We'll talk about it later.''

''Neither of you knows anything about me,'' Anna Lee said firmly, almost belligerently.

Henry looked at her in total surprise.

''What do you mean?'' he asked.

''I know what you were talking about, what you must have been talking about. And neither of you knows the answer.''

''To what question?'' Henry asked, but he knew what she was going to say. The anxious look on his face betrayed that.

''Neither of you knows whether I love you, or whether I still love Louis.''

"And what is the answer?" Henry asked. The words seemed forced up from somewhere down in his gut.

Anna Lee's fingertips brushed her auburn hair. "Henry, you haven't touched me since we got here."

"I know. If I touch you, I won't be able to stop."

Anna Lee swiveled halfway around in her chair, and with an inclination of her head, she pointed the way to the straw mattress, neatly fitted with a clean white linen sheet.

She turned back to Henry. Her fingers went back to her hair again; she untwisted the bun that she kept it up in, and it fell across her shoulders, rich and coppery and abundant. A breeze from the open door ruffled it with the same little flutter that suddenly touched Henry's heart, and ran up and down his spine.

"No one has asked you to stop, Henry," Anna Lee said in a voice that was no more than a whisper.

25

ANNA Lee walked over and closed the front door, then smiled apologetically at Henry.

"I know we're out in the middle of the forest, and there's no one else around for miles," she said. "But still . . ."

"Whatever you want," Henry said fervently.

Anna Lee stood with her back to the closed door, one hand pressed flat against, as if guarding their moment together from a treacherous, encroaching world. Slowly raising the other hand to her chest, she began to unbutton the buttons of her dress.

What was the answer?

Anna Lee thought she knew; but even she herself was not sure. She faced Henry across the length of the ruined cabin that she had been a little girl in, when all their lives had been as simple as the sun and snow and wind, the supply of beaver pelts and a dollar here and there from the pockets of travelers.

She was not a little girl any more. She was about to become a woman twice over, if this was what becoming a woman meant.

She draped her dress over the back of a chair, and walked slowly over to the mattress, watching him watch her walk. The expression on his face was sheer devotion, and Anna Lee allowed herself to enjoy it to the fullest extent.

She ran her hands down the side of her shift, smoothing it to the outline of her waist and hips shamelessly. *He's been in prison for months, now . . . he hasn't even seen a woman in all that time*, she thought. *Well, let him have a good time.*

But as she undid the bow and began to loosen the laces at the top of her shift, letting the cleft between her breasts widen to include more and more of their swelling roundness, she knew that she had only acknowledged a small part of what was in his eyes.

Jail or no jail, that look would have been there.

The shift dropped to her waist, and suddenly she felt shy. She crossed her arms over her breasts, and lowered her eyes.

He had not yet moved. He just kept looking at her, in the same way.

"Aren't you going to . . . you know . . .?"

She felt more naked under his gaze than any mere lack of clothing could ever have made her feel. He began walking toward her slowly, his arms up but not quite outstretched, his hands open, as if her were trying to hand-feed a tuft of grass or a tender green shoot to a shy wild deer.

"Anna Lee . . . oh, Anna Lee . . ." he repeated.

She had simply thought that she was going to marry him; she had not given much more thought to it. She did not understand how she could have missed it, but she had not known he was—she had not known that anyone could be—so much in love with her.

She looked into his eyes as he brought his body down over the length of hers, and was poised on the brink of entering her.

She thought in that instant of Louis, and of the passionate desire she had felt with him, the love and longing she had poured into him. And she remembered Louis's eyes. They had burned as brightly as the heart of a flame, but they had been like opaque glass, like a mirror that deflected everything back to her. Nothing could ever pass in or out.

In that instant, she decided she wanted to spend the rest of her life looking into eyes that knew how to look back at her.

Then he entered her. After that, she did no more thinking.

There was plenty of time to look into each other's eyes that afternoon, time to caress and make love and make love again, until the dusk gathered around them and their bodies lapsed languidly into a spent, happy state.

Anna Lee curled into Henry's body contentedly, and sighed, then half-opened her eyes and looked piqued. Henry was getting up, and walking away from her.

"Come back to bed, Henry," she coaxed.

Rummaging around in his saddlebag, Henry had found a candle and some matches. He lit the candle, and set it on the windowsill.

"What are you doing?" she asked. "Never mind the light. Come back to bed."

"We have to get up," he said.

"Why? That's silly."

"I should have told you before," Henry said in a boyishly guilty tone of voice."

"Told me what . . . *oh*!"

Suddenly the door smashed open, and a figure lurched into the room, snarling with rage. Standing in the doorway, he could only be seen in silhouette, but Anna Lee recognized her brother well enough.

"My God, James! What are you doing here? You told Mama you were on your way home," Anna Lee cried out, springing up to a sitting position and pulling a corner of the sheet over her as best she could.

"Whore!" James snarled at her. "I've caught you this time . . . both of you. Half-breed whore! You won't get away with this."

He held up something in his hands, and started waving it around the room. It was an Enfield repeating rifle, and he swung it back and forth between Anna Lee on the bed and Henry by the window.

"Got you with your pants down, Riel!" James said, not recognizing Sleight for who he was. "You filthy, fornicating half-breed swine! You're not going to get away this time!"

"James, that's not—"

"James, for God's sake, I'm—"

The crack of the rifle and an ugly spurt of light cut them both off.

Anna Lee screamed. But her scream died away in her throat, as she heard the cry of pain that came from the other side of the room.

And the two thuds: the first as Henry's body was thrown back against the wall by the force of the bullet, the second as it slid down the wall and finally fell heavily to the floor.

"You fool! Anna Lee hissed. "What have you done? You're crazy!"

Across the room from her, Henry moaned. "I'm hit . . . oh, God, Anna Lee, help me. God, it hurts . . ."

He tried to get up, but collapsed again. Anna Lee started over to him, but James was right over her, blocking her way.

"Let me past!" she blazed at him.

He spat in her face.

"Damn you, let me past, you madman!" she screamed. She clawed at his face, and he answered with a vicious back-of-the-hand slap that knocked her back down on the mattress, with points of light dancing in front of her eyes and her ears ringing.

"Whore!" he snarled. "Get back in bed, whore. That's the place for you. That's where you belong!"

Henry moaned again, but there was nothing Anna Lee could do for him. She was on her hands and knees, backing away from James, backing into the corner and crouching there, her body curled into a ball, looking up at him in utter terror.

His eyes glittered, and his teeth flashed. He really was crazy.

"What are you doing, James? What do you want from me? What are you going to do?"

"You're a disgrace," he told her. "You're my sister . . . you say you're my sister . . . but you're a disgrace to our whole family. You're a disgrace to our race. You're nothing but a half-breed's whore."

"James, listen to me, you don't understand. That's not even Louis . . ."

She did not know what difference that could possibly make. And he was not listening to her, anyway.

"My sister . . . they say you're my sister. I wonder. I

wonder if you really are. What do you say, sister dear? Are you really my sister?''

''James . . .''

''They say I'm a half-breed, you know. Have you heard that? The filthy liars say it behind my back. Have you heard anyone say it?''

''I don't . . .''

''Have you?''

''I may have . . .''

''It's a lie! It's a filthy, rotten lie. Isn't it a lie?''

''James, it doesn't make any difference . . .''

He bent down and hit her again, across the mouth. She felt a sharp pain first, and when the pain did not go away, she realized that her tooth had cut through her lower lip. She pushed the lip away carefully with her tongue, and disengaged it, but the pain went on, and blood trickled down her chin.

''Don't you ever say that! I'm white, as white as anyone whoever lived. Don't you dare say that. You're saying that Mama's a half-breed's whore like you! Is that what you're saying? Do you think Mama's a half-breed's whore?''

The blood was collecting at the point of Anna Lee's chin and falling, in single drops, into the cleft between her breasts.

''Is that what you're saying?''

''N . . . no, James.''

''You're damn right she's not. Mama's a saint. She doesn't deserve to have a whore like you for a daughter. A Goddamn half-breed's whore. Yes, maybe . . .''

He took a step closer to her. He was standing on the mattress now, standing on the white linen sheet, leaning on the barrel of his gun. He peered down at her, and a slow sneer spread across his face.

''You're the one who loves half-breeds so much. Maybe you're the half-breed.''

He did not notice his own contradiction. "My sister . . . why should you be my sister? They all think you're my half-sister anyway. And you are . . . that's the truth. You're the half-breed!"

James was raving now, driving himself from one mad fancy to another with the inevitability of a spring flood, while Anna Lee suddenly remembered—she had been so caught up in his madness, so afraid for Henry and afraid for her own life, that for a few moments she had not thought about it—she was naked.

She could not get to the sheet; he was still standing on it. She tried to cover up her body with her hands, and instantly realized that she had made a mistake.

James took up the gun in both hands again, and for an instant she thought he was going to shoot her. He pointed the barrel straight at her, the cold metal touching her breastbone.

Not to shoot, though. Sliding it down under her forearms where they were crossed over her breasts, he used it as a lever to pry them away. By this time, she knew better than to resist. As he giggled, she put her hands down to her sides.

She looked down at her breasts, and they were covered with her own blood. Her forearms were smeared with it, too.

It made her think of Henry. He was not moaning any more. She did not know whether he was still alive, and just unconscious, or . . .

James giggled again. She could feel his eyes on her body like clammy hands, or claws, or reptilian scales. It looked like such a poor thing to her, her own body, smeared with blood and mottled by goose bumps from the evening chill and her fear. The goose bumps around her nipples were as big as the nipples; why would anyone want such a body? It should be swept aside, set in the corner of a closet someplace, and just forgotten about until it could be mended later. Surely no one could have any use for it, now.

"Half-breed whore . . . yeah, you love it, don't you? Just like an animal. You're an animal, that's what you are . . . you're a filthy animal half-breed and I'm white through and through! I know what you want. You want me to fuck you. Well, don't think I'd do such a disgusting thing. I'm civilized, I am. I'm saving myself in the sight of God . . . and Mama . . . I wouldn't soil my dick by putting it in the likes of you."

He poked her hard, in the pit of her stomach, with the rifle, so that she groaned with pain.

"All right, what are you waiting for? Lie down on your back!"

"No!"

Blind panic overcame her, and she blocked everything out of her mind except getting away. She dove past him, momentarily catching him off guard, hit the floor rolling, and got to her feet. Her hand was on the doorlatch when he caught her again. He hit her with a wild swing to the back of the neck, and her face and breasts were smashed hard against the door.

He seized her by the shoulder and turned her around roughly, pinning her against the door first with one hand and then with his body.

"Don't run away from me, you whore," he panted. "Don't ever . . . run . . . away from . . ."

He kissed her hard on her sore, bruised mouth, grinding his face against hers. She could not breathe, and she was sure that her jaw was going to be crushed, by the time he released her, only to spin her around and fling her violently across the room. She stumbled backwards, and fell back down onto the mattress.

"Don't move," he commanded her, and then his voice took on, for a moment, an insanely playful lilt. "All I want is a little loving . . . just like you give every . . . *don't move or I'll kill you.*"

There was no chance of her moving, anyway. She was beaten, and she could do no more than to lie there and wish she were dead, while she watched him begin to unbutton his fly.

As he reached the third button, he put his left hand down inside his pants; and it was while he was in that position that the door caught him, as it crashed open with terrific force, and Louis Riel charged into the cabin.

Hopelessly off balance, James went crashing to the floor, landing on the point of his left shoulder. He seemed to be having trouble moving his arm, but he twitched over and had risen back up to his knees, when Louis landed on him again with a flying leap.

They rolled over on the floor together, near to where Anna Lee lay, half on and half off the mattress, and she scrambled back from them and tucked her legs away from the range of their thrashing, as if she were moving back up the shore of a lake to avoid the incoming, lapping waves.

Louis was on top, but James was still struggling, clawing at his face and trying to bring his knee up into Louis's groin or stomach. Then Louis pinned his arms and legs, and for a second, their bodies were frozen, and there was no sound except for the harsh rasping of breath.

Is it over? Anna Lee wondered, but James pulled loose again, and shoved Louis backward as he wrenched his shoulder and forearm into Louis's chest. Louis sprang on top of him again, and this time, Anna Lee saw his arm swing up in the air, and the blade of a knife glinting in his hand.

The blade came down in a short arc. When it rose again, it was no longer glinting: the dull color of blood made it hard to pick out against the background of shadow. It went down again, in another short arc, and this time it did not come up.

26

JAMES was dead. Henry was alive. The bullet, at such short range, had gone clean through his shoulder and imbedded itself in the wall, but the bone had been badly broken.

While Anna Lee bathed his wound, Louis searched around for materials to make a splint and sling. Henry woke up while Louis was setting the bone in place, and signalled his return to consciousness with a blood-curdling scream.

"This may hurt a bit," Louis said.

"It just did," Henry answered groggily. He was beginning to pull himself together, though, and he only winced and sucked in his breath as Louis began to wrap bandages around him.

"Not very Spartan, that, was it?" he apologized. "I'll try to do better."

"Just sit up, so I can bandage you," Louis grunted. "Anna Lee, you help him. From the back."

They had Henry lying on the mattress, covered by the half of the sheet which had not been torn up for bandages. As Anna Lee pushed him up into a sitting position, it slid off his body.

Louis quickly pulled it up and tucked it fastidiously around Henry's waist. Then he went back to wrapping the bandages around his chest and shoulder.

A shot of brandy would have been helpful, but there was none. They made Henry as comfortable as possible under the circumstances, and only then did Anna Lee finally turn to Louis, and ask:

"How on earth did you happen to be up here?"

Louis turned his head away. "Maybe I shouldn't have come," he said dourly.

"What do you mean, you shouldn't have come?" Anna Lee responded incredulously. "You saved our lives!"

Louis continued to look away, and Anna Lee suddenly became aware, for the first time, of the nakedness that had been her condition when Louis first arrived.

She had put her dress on while Louis still lay panting over James's body, reflexively, even before she had run over to Henry. She blushed deeply with belated embarrassment.

"I asked him to meet us out here," Henry said.

"You did what? Why?"

"You remember what you said before—that neither of us knew anything about you, including which one of us you really loved? Well, we knew that. We talked about it, when we were talking about you. I didn't . . . I didn't want you to be forced by circumstance into going off with me, if it were Riel you really loved. I wanted to be fair to you. So I asked him to meet us out here. I thought the three of us could talk it over."

Anna Lee stared at Henry, openmouthed. Riel had turned his back.

"I was just starting to tell you. I'd put the candle in the window as a signal to Riel, when he got here, that we were here and he was to come in. I was only trying to be fair to everybody. I thought we should talk."

Anna Lee sighed. "Someday, Henry Sleight, when your shoulder is healed, and when I've finished thanking God ten times every day for sending Louis here when we needed him, I am going to be very angry with you."

There was nothing to talk about. Not as far as Louis Riel was concerned, anyway. Whether it was his pride or his prudishness that was injured, Anna Lee was not sure. But she knew Louis well enough to know that his mood would not be mollified.

He was going to take James's body back to Fort Garry with him.

Henry tried to talk him out of it. "Leave him here. We'll bury him; we'll tell Mrs. Graham he met with an accident. How can it help your cause to come riding into Fort Garry with a dead boy?"

"He was a felon, an escaped prisoner, and a rebel against the established government and its laws. We are a legal government, and we have the legal right to impose laws and sanctions."

And he was going to leave right away.

"In the dark? With a . . . with that kind of burden? You ought to stay," Anna Lee implored him.

He would not talk to her at all.

It broke her heart. She wanted them to be friends; she wanted him to know that she would always cherish him in her heart. She wondered, as she watched him ride off into the night, and listened to the sound of his horse's hooves long after the darkness had swallowed him up, if she would ever see him again.

EPILOGUE

DR. John Schultz had been right. Louis Riel had gone too far. In Canadian circles, while the murder of a half-witted *métis* boy by a gang of whites might go unnoticed, the killing by a *métis* of the son of one of the areas most prominent whites was a cause for considerable concern—especially among those who had just been waiting for the chance to brand Louis Riel as a renegade and a pirate.

By this time, a delegation from Riel's provisional Red River government was already in Ottawa, working out an agreement with MacDonald's government. The agreement became law—the Manitoba Act of May, 1870, which provided for the annexation of the Red River settlement into the dominion of Canada as the new province of Manitoba, with full legal rights guaranteed to all its citizens, regardless of race, creed, or color.

But by the time the delegation returned to Winnipeg to present the terms of the agreement to the provisional government, MacDonald, under heavy pressure from Dr. John

Schultz's lobby, had sent a force of arms marching on Red River: 100 men, commanded by Colonel Garnet Wolseley, a veteran of colonial campaigns in Burma, India, the Crimea, and China.

Wolseley knew how to deal with rebels, although he was somewhat tempered in his plans by the awareness that his technique could be overstepping the bounds that MacDonald had laid out for him. "In a way, I hope Riel will have bolted by the time we get there," he wrote his wife. "For although I should like to hang him from the highest tree in the place, I have such a horror of rebels and vermin of this kidney, that my treatment of him might not be approved by the civil powers."

The Manitoba Act was read to the Legislative Assembly of the provisional government in June, and a motion to accept its terms passed by acclamation.

The Red River settlement—the province of Manitoba—was a part of Canada. The provisional government had won its battle, and it was ready to retire from the field. The *métis* provisional army disbanded, and its soldiers went home to farm or hunt. Louis Riel and his lieutenants stayed on at Fort Garry as a caretaker government, to formally hand over authority to the new Lieutenant Governor as soon as he arrived.

Wolseley's army was traveling overland from Lake Superior; the government of the United States had forbidden them access to the American route. They did not arrive in Manitoba until late August.

On August 21, they reached Lake Winnipeg, and by August 22, their supply boats were on the Red River. Wolseley had tried to conduct the march in secret, arresting *métis* whom they passed on the way and whom they suspected might get the word through to Riel; but word got through anyway.

Riel sent scouts out. They never came back. They, too, were taken prisoner by Wolseley's army. And the next evening, the smoke from their campfires could be seen six miles outside of Fort Garry.

It rained all that night, and the next morning, Wolseley's troops did their best to imitate a triumphal march through the quagmires that led to the fort.

"A few stray inhabitants in the village declared that Riel and his party still held possession of the fort," one of Wolseley's men, a Captain Huyshe, would write later, "and that they meant to fight. The gates were shut, and guns were visible, mounted in the bastions and over the gateway that commanded the approach from the village and the prairie over which the troops were advancing.

"It certainly looked as if our labors were not to be altogether in vain. 'Riel is going to fight!' ran along the line, and the men quickened their pace and strode cheerily forward, regardless of the mud and rain. M. Riel rose in their estimation immensely.

"The gun over the Main Gate was expected at every moment to open fire, but we got nearer and nearer and still no sign; at last we could see that there were no men standing to the guns, and, unless it were a trap to get us close up before they opened fire, it was evident that there would be no fight after all. 'My God!' He's bolted!' went the cry.

"Colonel Wolseley sent forward some of his men to see if the south gate were also shut; they galloped all around the fort, and brought back word that the gate opening onto the bridge over the Assiniboine River was wide open, and men were bolting away over the bridge. The troops then marched in by this gateway, and took possession of Fort Garry.

"This was a sad disappointment to the soldiers, who, having gone through so much toil in order to put down the rebellion, longed to be avenged on its authors."

Colonel Wolseley, on the other hand, looked at the bright side.

"Personally," he told his troops, "I was glad that Riel did not come out and surrender as he had at one time said he would, for I could not then have hanged him as I will now be able to, when he is chased down and apprehended as a rebel in arms against his sovereign."

Wolseley would not catch Riel, and he could not banish with him the legal and constitutional rights that Riel had won for all the people of Manitoba. But the implementation of those rights would not come right away. First, a new government was installed under an interim Lieutenant Governor, Louis Cameron, who had come out with Wolseley.

Cameron's administration produced exactly one official act: he signed a warrant for the arrest of Louis Riel.

Beyond that, he left Manitoba in the hands of the newly arrived peace-keeping forces. Within three days, all the liquor in Winnipeg was gone.

Merchants from Minnesota were quickly on the scene with more; and to the tune of rape, looting, and drunken violence, Canadian law and order entered the province of Manitoba.

Dr. John Schultz was back in town. He came in with the first shipment of whiskey, reopened his store, and within a week, given the law of supply and demand for liquor in Winnipeg, he had made up for all the lost profits he had suffered when his store had been closed during the rule of the provisional government.

Schultz did better than that, within the year. The Canadian government appointed a federal judge to assess claims for damages incurred during the Canadian acquisition of the Northwest. Schultz put in for, and won without question, a claim for $65,000.

Charlotte Graham came away with $30,000; no one else was even close.

Henry Sleight might have put in a claim. He had hung on in Red River, and risked his life, to protect that investment. But he chose not to.

"No, I couldn't," he told Anna Lee. "I was wrong. And doubly at fault for not getting out immediately, once I knew I was wrong."

They had come to Ottawa with nothing, as Henry had sworn they would not. But he was not as devoid of resources as he had feared. He had his reputation as a writer, and a reputation for knowledge of the problems of the Northwest, and he accepted a position in the Ministry of the Interior. Later that year, as reports of the chaos under Cameron came in to MacDonald, he called Henry Sleight and offered him the lieutenant governorship.

"I'm afraid I can't accept, sir."

"Why not, man? It's a promotion beyond your wildest expectations. And you're the perfect man for the job. You're young, vigorous, and you have a feeling for the frontier. And you know both factions out there."

"And both factions hate and distrust me."

"That's all right. They'd hate and mistrust anyone who does a good job."

"I can't accept, sir. I've lost my feeling for the frontier. And I couldn't ask my wife to go back. You know that her brother was killed out there."

"Hm, yes. By that madman, Riel."

"Precisely, sir."

* * *

He told Anna Lee about the conversation that night, when they were in the big four-poster bed in the master bedroom of their brick house in Ottawa. She listened, as she pulled the eiderdown quilt up under her armpits, then reached down and patted her stomach through it.

"It means I passed up a tremendous salary increase and some significant amount of power," he told her. "I hope you don't mind."

"You'll get them both in time," she said. "Do I mind? I don't want Henry, Jr., to ever *see* Fort Garry."

Then she rolled over and threw her arms around him.